DEVIL'S PLAY

SARAH SHERIDAN

ALSO BY SARAH SHERIDAN

For Bev, Isabella, Milla, Ginny and George; here's to another thirty years of friendship.

1

———

Shirley Butterworth opened one eye. The scene in front of her – the result of last night's attempt to numb her searing hurt and rejection with three bottles of red wine – prompted her to quickly shut it again. What she'd spied in a second or two were three empty wine bottles, two on their sides on the coffee table and one on the floor, five empty packets of crisps, a plethora of crumbs, and a wine glass that was also lying haphazardly on the floor. It must have rolled off her lap at some point when she'd passed out. An unwelcome slicing pain, that seemed keen to split her head in two, made her flinch. She appeared to have morphed into the sofa and become one with it – and was pretty sure she was still in the exact position she'd been in when falling into an alcoholic coma – not that she could remember doing so. Much of her mass of frizzy, ginger hair – uncontrollable since birth – hung over her face. Her neck ached and so did her back. She let out a deep groan. Damn and bugger it, she hadn't got that drunk for years. Okay, maybe for months. Possibly weeks. And it was all bloody Tiffany's fault for leaving. For saying those unforgettable words that had stabbed her in the heart and made her bleed vulnerability. Feeling so ripped apart and weak had been unbearable, intolerable, and the moment Tiffany had slammed the front door shut after dragging her bulging suitcase through it, Shirley had headed to the wine rack and grabbed as many bottles as she could carry. For the love of God, she thought, what kind of private detective allowed themselves to be such an emotional mess in the evenings? No wonder she wasn't getting much work at the moment. Perhaps potential clients could sniff her internal unravelling from miles away, even before they picked up the phone to call.

Footsteps upstairs made her groan again. Bloody Noah would be down in a minute, staring at her in his serious way, making his habitual entirely sensible but irritating observations. She wondered yet again about her decision to take her eccentric nephew in. But how could she say no to her distraught sister, who was so worried about her socially-awkward seventeen-year-old son? Noah was permanently threatening to leave his college course in chemistry, and Shirley lived practically on top of the Winslow campus where he was enrolled. Gloria had begged her, pleaded with her, to let Noah stay with her – just for a bit – to see if she could entice him to walk the two hundred yards to college every day. It was to be a last-ditch attempt at keeping him in education, after Gloria had discovered that Noah had started skipping classes, apparently preferring to go to the library to read science fiction books all day rather than further his knowledge of the complex chemical world. Privately, Shirley had wondered why Gloria was trying to make her son do something he clearly didn't want to do – there were loads of other pathways into work these days, weren't there? But her sister seemed to have faith in Shirley's exterior tough no-nonsense approach to life, so she'd grudgingly agreed to give it a try. Perhaps Gloria would have reconsidered if she knew what a mess Shirley actually was in on the *inside*...

'Oh, you got drunk again.' Noah's pale face, shrouded in the long greasy hair he refused to cut, appeared at the door. 'Do you have a hangover?'

'Oh fuck off, Noah,' Shirley said with a sigh, opening one eye again. 'Anyway, why aren't you at college? It must be well past registration time by now.' She attempted to focus on the clock on the wall. It seemed to say quarter past eleven, but as she currently had alcohol-induced double vision she couldn't be sure.

Noah walked in and folded his lanky frame into the armchair opposite her.

'I've decided to leave college,' he said. 'I mean it this time.'

Shirley let out a strangled noise.

'Oh come on, not this bullshit again,' she said, opening the other eye and shifting her gigantic frame into a more upright position. 'We've been through this too many times now, Noah. Cut the crap, get your bag, and piss off to learn about the periodic table.'

'I learnt the periodic table when I was seven, Shirley. At college we're learning about kinetic molecular theory.' Noah looked at her, his face without guile, as always.

Shirley rolled her eyes, a gesture she immediately regretted after it brought on another stab in her head.

'Whatever. Go and learn about that then.'

'There's no point.' Noah shook his head.

'Why?'

'I already know more than the teacher.' Noah's forehead creased.

'That's a bit arrogant, isn't it, Noah?' Shirley said, while privately suspecting it was probably true. 'Anyway, don't you want to hang out with your friends?' She knew she was clutching at straws with that comment, but it was worth a shot.

'I don't have any friends,' Noah said simply.

Shirley groaned.

'By the way, your mascara is really smudged under your eyes.' Noah squinted at her. 'It's a total mess. And look, you spilt red wine on the carpet – you'll never get that out.'

'Fuck off, Noah,' Shirley said again, refusing to look down at where he was gesturing. 'Okay, so why don't you have any friends? Don't you want any?'

'Not really,' Noah said in his clipped tones. 'I find most of my age group annoying.'

Shirley stared at him. God, why did he have to be so weird? Mind you, coming from the family they did, he'd got off lightly. Ever since her father had had a breakdown and hung himself when she was fourteen, she had known she was doomed genetically. Her younger sister Gloria was all right, although admittedly was bordering on neurotic at the moment. Their older sister Sally had always been unhinged, and Shirley had lost count of the times she'd tried to top herself over the years. Their mother Rose was a stubborn, prejudiced old bitch, who'd thrown cushions across the room and screamed when Shirley had finally plucked up the courage twenty years ago to come out as gay to her, at the ripe old age of twenty-five. 'Why are you doing this to me?' Rose had snarled. 'Don't you know people round here think well of me? What will they think now? Don't tell anyone. You'll probably grow out of it.' At which point Shirley had gone out and got drunk, and told as many people as possible.

'Your mum will kill me if you stop going to college, Noah,' Shirley said, deciding to try and guilt him into understanding how much she didn't want to incur the neurotic wrath of his mum Gloria. 'You know how worried she is about you.'

'I'm seventeen, Shirley,' Noah said. 'In the old days I would be out at work now. In fact, if I was a chimney sweep I'd have been employed since the age of four.'

'Yes, but you're not a shitting chimney sweep, are you, Noah?'

Shirley said with a growl. 'You're a dysfunctional young man who's about to throw his prospects away.'

Noah cleared his throat.

'Not if I'm employed by you, Shirley. I've decided I want to be a private investigator. I want to work with you.' He sat back, his eyes brighter than usual, watching her.

'You what?'

'Don't try and change my mind,' he said, his voice containing an unusual firmness. 'I've thought about this a lot, and watched you take on cases and work through them. You've really helped some people. Not that you've had many jobs recently, which is probably due to the fact that you are an alcoholic. That sort of thing puts people off. You need an assistant, Shirley. Look at the state of your desk, it looks like more of a junkyard than the rest of the room, and that's saying something.'

They both glanced over at the dark mahogany writing bureau in the corner of the living room, the only thing Shirley had inherited from granddad Pete after he'd passed away. He'd been the one to bring his family up to Buckinghamshire from London's East End all those years ago 'for a better life'. Her mum and her siblings had stayed ever since, spawning a variety of mostly misfit-type children and grandchildren. Fine, so the open desk currently had masses of papers – some crumpled – dripping off the sides. And on top of the papers were a mess of files, books and assorted stationery items. All right, so organisation wasn't at the top of her list of qualities, Shirley internally acquiesced. And maybe she did need an assistant. But there was no bloody way she could afford one.

'I don't want paying while I'm an apprentice,' Noah said, as though reading her mind. 'Not for the first year, at least, while I'm learning the ropes. After that, I'm sure we can work something out.'

Shirley glared at him, surprised to find she was actually considering his unexpected proposition.

'By the way,' she said after a minute or two. 'I'll have you know that I'm not an alcoholic, actually, Noah. I was just very upset after Tiffany left last night. But then you wouldn't understand about relationships.'

'No,' Noah said. 'Maybe not. But I do understand that you use alcohol as an emotional crutch when you are stressed. Or bored. Or upset, or if you have any feelings you find difficult.'

'Oh shut up,' Shirley said quietly, shifting fully upright, a difficult manoeuvre because whenever she moved the room swam in front of her. *The little git's right though*, she admitted silently. *Damn him.* She took a big breath in, then let out a long sigh.

'Gloria's not going to be happy about this.' She shook her head. 'She's going to have my guts for garters, Noah. She really wants you to continue in education, you know?'

'She'll get over it,' Noah said. 'In time. Especially if I help you make this practice really successful, which I'm pretty sure I will do. So will you take me on, Shirley? I can start by tidying your desk? You know I'm good at ordering things. I actually enjoy it.'

Shirley lowered her eyebrows, thinking of Noah's spartan bedroom upstairs. He'd been staying in her box room for nearly four months now, during which time she'd seen him carefully alphabetise his numerous books, array his pens across his desk with mathematical precision, hoover his carpet daily, as well as go out and buy cleaning products with the pocket money Gloria provided him with. He'd scrubbed the little room so much it now smelt like a disinfectant factory, which was annoying, as it highlighted the fact that the rest of the house didn't.

'Oh God,' she said. 'I can't believe I'm actually going to say this, Noah, and I'm probably still drunk, but fine. I'll take you on for a trial period of three months. However, if it doesn't work out you have to go back to college without any more fuss. Agreed?'

Noah smiled a rare smile.

'Thank you, Shirley. You won't regret it, I promise. Right, I'll make a start on your desk straight away.' He stood up.

I'm already bloody regretting it, Shirley thought as she let her aching eyelids close again. She tried unsuccessfully to block out the scene Gloria would make when she told her that Noah was leaving college – albeit probably temporarily – to become her assistant. Damn the boy, it was enough to make her want another glass of red.

'Oh and by the way, I'm hiding the rest of the wine,' Noah called. 'You've had quite enough of that for now. Anyway, you'll probably die if you drink any more today, and then I'll never get my training.'

Bollocks, Shirley thought. *Damn, bugger and shit.*

2

On the day of her death, Eleanor Parkhurst's eyes flickered open and as her mind clicked into gear, a slow, wide smile broke out across her lips. It was Wednesday at last, she realised, *finally* here after six whole dragging days. A thrill of excitement rushed through her body and she wriggled under her pink covers, enjoying the feeling. Not long to wait now. Her eyes flicked towards her alarm clock, and the neon digits flashed 12.47pm back at her. There was just over seven hours to go. It was lunchtime, but she doubted she'd be able to eat much today, not with what she had to look forward to later...

It was a miracle she'd managed to get through the last week at all, she reflected, rolling onto her back. She stretched out her long, slender limbs, and a shaft of pale light slithering through the thick university curtains made her golden hair glow. One way or another she'd managed to bear every long hour of clock-watching, every minute of phone-checking; she'd forced herself to sit through every tutorial and lecture – well, most of them anyway. And somehow she'd managed to finish the dreaded essay about Matisse's use of colour last night; it must have been past 3am when she'd finally closed her laptop. The writing and content wasn't up to her usual standard, she already knew that, but she didn't care. It had felt like an endurance task rather than her usual enjoyment of the immersion in the subject matter. She'd emailed the paper off to her tutor Daniel anyway in the small hours of the morning – without checking through it – and wasn't looking forward to the caustic comments that would no doubt be plastered across it on its return.

Professor Daniel Weatherby could be a taskmaster at the best of times, she thought, rolling her eyes. Lauded throughout the academic community for his incisive analysis of art, he always kept his class of four masters' students on their toes with his relentless expectations; continuously willing them to go above and beyond what they thought they were capable of in their research. Although at least when he praised someone, that person knew he meant it. Half the time Eleanor wished she was getting an easier ride in Doctor Abigail Dahiru's class. The only other art lecturer at the smallish university, Abigail was – according to other students – much more approachable.

'Let's meet up at the Horse and Hounds on Friday after class,' Eleanor had heard Abigail saying to her tutor group as they'd exited her study one day. 'It would be great for us to get to know each other more outside the academic environment, don't you think?'

Daniel would never do that, he was all business and no play. A nose-to-the-grindstone kind of guy. Although granted, Abigail apparently spent a portion of each tutorial asleep; being a working mother to five smallish children constantly zapped her energy and she was famous for her naps, which seemingly occurred anywhere at any time. But she was also known to be kind and encouraging. Whereas Daniel was ferocious and unforgiving. But also brilliant and highly-regarded. Ah well, at least he was better than the head of the arts faculty, Professor Eric Van Bern; the way that man had stared at her ever since she'd arrived at the Royal Buckingham University made her skin crawl. She remembered how full of excitement she'd been on her first day two months ago, so eager to start her master's in modernist art, full of anticipation at the adventure ahead. Then sitting back in the lecture hall and wondering why the head of faculty wouldn't take his eyes from her. Yep, there sure was something lechy about Van Bern, but in a distant way, he never did or said anything inappropriate to her. In fact he'd barely spoken to her at all. It was just something about his eyes that creeped her out.

Up until a fortnight ago, Eleanor mused, she'd been fully engaged with her degree, keeping up with the essay deadlines and attending all her lectures; even earning praise from Daniel for her analysis of Braque's Cubist work and her presentation on Picasso. She'd also grabbed many moments to enjoy her on-off dalliance with Seth. But since meeting Dillon Rushwell, all of that now seemed boring, an unwelcome distraction that got in the way of her new, obsessive fantasising. How could she not constantly think about this unbelievable, dynamic human being – who'd just entered her life like a bolt of lightning? And now Wednesday was here at last, and she would get to see Dillon again in just a few hours. The enigmatic man who'd so successfully captured her mind and heart in the way nobody had managed before.

She sat up, shaking out her duvet quickly so that the freezing November air – always seeping through the old bricks and unsealed windows – didn't ruin her cosy warm nest, enjoying the way the quilt's heavy weight sank deliciously back down on top of her legs. She'd always loved different types of caressing sensations on her skin, and was hoping that tonight would lead to more of that in multiple ways with Dillon...

The temperature around her face and neck turned even colder, momentarily pulling her out of her reverie. Bloody crap old heating, she thought, leaning over the side of the bed in search of her dressing gown. A stab of exasperation rippled through her as a freezing blast crept under her cover. Had anything at all been updated in the uni halls since the building had been built three hundred years previously? It certainly didn't feel like it. The mansion had been built in the eighteenth century by an old boy named Lord Hugo Arbuthnot – she remembered Daniel informing her class all about it on their induction day in a bored kind of voice.

'As you can tell, Lord Arbuthnot liked spending his inheritance on superficial monuments,' he'd said with a drawl. 'Enjoyed impressing his friends. They vied to see who could have the most architecture in their gardens.'

He'd obviously been told to give them some history of the building, but didn't relish doing it as it wasn't about art. The Royal Buckingham University had been the proprietor of the whole estate for the past twenty-five years, including all of its various higgledy-piggledy buildings that spread out across the rolling grounds. Lord Arbuthnot had certainly had a penchant for random bits of architecture. There were tons of old, crumbling temples, shrines, grottos, arches, tiny chapels – as well as lots of ponds – punctuating the grassy acres, as well as the more traditional enormous mansion, converted stables and adjoining cottages – with the halls of residence, lecture theatres, studies and classrooms all situated in the latter three. Perhaps it would be a good idea if the uni spent some of the revenue earned from the extortionate fees they charged on upgrading the plumbing, Eleanor thought, rather than constantly attempting to repair the old dude's crazy stone creations. Saying that though, she had to admit that the grounds were exceptionally beautiful; they were what had attracted her to the university in the first place. There was something enchanting about them, especially first thing in the morning, or at sunset.

Silently thanking her dad for splashing out on a substantial new bedding set at the beginning of the autumn term, she retrieved the dressing gown from under her bed and quickly stuffed her arms inside, before wrapping the fleecy softness around herself. Dad had always been practical like that, bless him. Always giving her gifts that would make her everyday life a bit easier. He'd always treated his only child like a princess, it seemed to make him happy. He ordered everything on his laptop nowadays, of course, avoided leaving the house whenever he could. It made her sad to think about how he'd withdrawn from life over the years, hating having to use his wheelchair, his head drooping with what – shame? –whenever she went with him to the shops. Going out in public seemed to make him more dejected, he was always very quiet for a while after they got home. He hadn't always been like that, only since the crash... Anyway, she wasn't thinking about any of that today, was she? There was no room for bad memories or sadness right now; not when she had such an exciting – albeit arctic – evening to look forward to.

For a moment Eleanor imagined showing Dillon into her room for the first time. She wondered if he'd ever been inside a girl's room in the halls before. Last week, when she'd chatted to him at the end of their session, trying to find out as much as she could about him while still appearing casual and unbothered, he'd said he didn't actually attend the uni. He'd said he was employed as the caretaker and handyman, and lived in a small cottage on the edge of the thickly wooded grounds. His job was to attend to the general upkeep of the place, and fix anything that needed attention. But the staff at the uni knew him well – he was a known face around town – and let him run an unusual but popular club in the old ruined temple. Dillon called this group New Satanism, and had apparently assured the staff – at the time of setting it up – that it wasn't about worshipping the

Devil, but more about using the Devil as a symbol that reflected rebelliousness over pointless authority. He'd said the role play involved would help students gain confidence and a sense of individualism, and to teach them to think about who they really were and what they believed. He'd also pointed out it was discriminatory not to allow the club to exist, since there were other Christian clubs at the university who denounced the Devil. He'd argued – successfully as it turned out – that the club was necessary for the freedom of speech and thought, and needed to run concurrently with other religious clubs that told students what to think and believe, contesting that his club taught people to question everything they'd been told to have blind faith in. It was progressive, he'd explained, a new and different type of political and religious club. So the liberal university had allowed him to run it. The fact that this group turned out to have much more dangerous connotations was still something Eleanor was trying to get her head around. She'd been shocked when she'd first realised what was really going on, but not repelled. It had made her curious, excited even...

She hadn't found out Dillon's age yet, but if she had to guess Eleanor would put him mid to late twenties. Older than her, which was a bonus, as she'd been fantasising about being with a more experienced, mature man for some time. Boys her own age – twenty-two – were basically annoying, they just wanted to get drunk with their mates all the time, which was super boring. She imagined that Dillon wouldn't be like that; he didn't look the type. And she already knew he was great at conversation.

But she was kidding herself if she thought he'd never slept with a girl in her halls before, she reflected, turning over. He'd probably visited the rooms here on multiple occasions. In fact, he was so gorgeous, girls probably threw themselves at him wherever he went. Well, Eleanor was classier than that; she had always refused to appear desperate to any man. Even if she was.

And anyway, she had other more stylish methods of attracting his attention, all ready and waiting to be deployed.

Wow, it felt good to have this secret, the one that she'd told no one about. Not her friends, not her dad, and definitely not her puppy-dog admirer Seth, who'd become annoyingly clingy lately, bless his little heart. She'd have to gently disentangle herself from Seth, in a way that kept him as a friend but not a lover. She was good at that. She smiled to herself; she'd had enough practise. In fact, she'd already started the process; he'd wanted to spend last night with her but she'd declined with a smile and a kiss, explaining she had the essay to finish. Because tonight – at the New Satanism Society she'd joined just two weeks before – she was going to see the Adonis that was Dillon, and it had never been her style to play two people along at the same time. Well, okay, so there had been slight overlaps in her dating history before, but that wasn't her fault; she couldn't exactly stare into the future and predict when she was going to meet someone new and more exciting, could she?

The fact that she was going to see Dillon wasn't in itself unknown to anybody. There would be other people at the meeting, too, of course; fellow initiates who attended the ruined temple in Royal Buckingham University's grounds every Wednesday at 8pm, ready for their two hours of ritual and role play. Seth said Dillon had a good nose for sniffing people out, that he could read them – almost in a psychic way, and knew after an initial meeting whether or not they should be admitted to the group. Apparently he'd never been wrong, and his followers were unflinchingly loyal; no one questioned his increasingly dark claims.

Eleanor's secret – the thing that absolutely *no one* knew – was that she'd fallen in love with Dillon; had become obsessed and intoxicated by him, to the point where he was all she thought about from the moment she awoke until the moment she fell asleep. And even then she dreamed about him, about what they would do together, about how they would make each other feel. Was it crazy to feel like this about someone she hardly knew? No; otherwise the saying 'love at first sight' wouldn't exist. She'd never been one to publicly let on about the depth of her feelings for someone, she played those cards close to her chest, and she had no intention of changing that now. Openly flirting, yes. But the deeper feeling of love – now that was private, hers alone to enjoy. She'd never told a man, other than her father, that she loved him, even if she felt the mild stirrings of it within her. But this powerful, all-consuming sensation she felt for Dillon was different. Would he be the first person she opened up to? Admitted her feelings for? Only time would tell...

She grinned, a stab of lust trembling through her body. The fact that Dillon was edgy – a bad boy who headed up a Satanic society – was definitely part of his appeal. Everything about him was addictive, he literally oozed with charm and mystery. Her poor father would quake in his wheelchair if he knew how she felt about this man – and more to the point if he knew she'd become involved with the sadly misunderstood Satanic movement – but he never would, Eleanor would make sure of that. She was good at keeping secrets; after all, she'd had to learn that craft from an early age, hadn't she? Her mother's troubles had made sure of that. Dillon's rock-hard biceps – always on show as he seemed to only ever wear sleeveless black T-shirts and ripped skinny jeans even when it was freezing – his beautiful, almost effeminately perfect face, his long brown hair – usually wound up in a loose top knot, his exotic tattoo sleeves, his eyebrow and nose piercings and his sexy eyes, that seemed to see into straight into her soul. She had to have him, she wouldn't rest until she had. Surely it was only a matter of time now...

Eleanor giggled, the excitement of it all making her tingle. She didn't usually have much trouble enticing any man she fancied, she knew she was good at making the target of her choice fall for her within hours, or days at the very least. She knew she was beautiful; her naturally blonde hair, full deep-red lips, smoky blue eyes and porcelain skin had always been a hit with the opposite sex. She'd been twelve – and tall for her age – when a man had whistled at her for the first time, slowing down on his motorbike to stare. She remembered being surprised but pleased at the time, and she'd felt a sense of power. Her looks had enticed a feeling of desire in someone, and she'd enjoyed playing on that possibility ever since. Anyway, what harm did it do to flirt with men? They loved it, and she revelled in their attention, so it was a win–win situation for everyone involved. The ability to complement her looks with charm was a trick she'd learnt at a young age, watching her adoptive socialite mother Diana wrap men round her finger with a glance, a blush, a softly spoken phrase. She'd always tried to ignore and forget the look on her father's face as he watched his wife charm so many others.

'Charles said I get prettier every year,' she remembered her mother giggling on the way back from one of the garden parties they were always going to. Her father's face hadn't shown quite so much amusement though. He'd never been able to stop his wife's affairs, and he'd loved her too much to leave. Which was probably why he'd focused all his attention on Eleanor, wanting and willing her to always be the perfect daughter. That was back then, of course, before the accident that changed everything. But she wasn't thinking about that horrendous incident today, was she?

Dillon was different to any other man she'd ever met. He was already playing mind games with her as much as she was with him. They'd known each other for exactly fourteen days, but he wasn't acting like most men did towards her. Even when she'd begun to scale up her charm levels last week, he hadn't fully fallen into her power like men normally did, and this was beyond intriguing. She could tell he was interested, but she couldn't fully reel him in. He'd sent the odd text to her over the last week, after she'd asked for his number, saying she wanted to find out more about New Satanism. But he hadn't bombarded her like men usually did. It was like they'd each taken on the roles of both cat and mouse, sometimes verbally toying with each other, at other times being the victim of the game. Dillon clearly wasn't going to roll over quickly like the besotted Seth had – who now followed her everywhere around uni, showering her with endless compliments and gifts. Seth was nice, of course he was. But he was too predictable. His idea of a good night out was going out and getting hammered, then going back to one of their friend's rooms in the halls to play on the PlayStation. Seth didn't live in the halls with the rest of them, he couldn't afford it, had to stay at his mum's house in Buckingham town, so when he wasn't staying in her room he usually crashed on other people's floors. Another problem was that he was nearly three years younger than her, only nineteen, and it was starting to make her feel like a cradle-snatcher. With Dillon she knew it would be a long game, and she couldn't wait. The anticipation of it was almost too much to bear. And she'd bet her whole make-up bag that he didn't own a PlayStation.

She'd lost count of the amount of nights she'd spent watching Seth and their other mates – well, Seth's friends really, she'd just kind of morphed into the group when she'd got to know him – play mind-numbing car and football games. How on earth they found it interesting, she didn't know. She'd been surprised that Hunter, a great beast of a man and a mature student who was thirty-one, liked playing the games as much as Seth. She'd tried to get on with Hunter's girlfriend Natalie, but the girl was a closed book, and hardly spoke to her, rarely smiling at all. Ah well, Eleanor had always had more male friends than female so she wasn't going to lose any sleep over Natalie's coldness. They all had one thing in common though, that they *did* talk about together, and that was New Satanism.

It had been Seth who'd introduced her to Dillon's society. Poor Seth, who so badly wanted to be a big player in life but probably never would be, who'd had a terrible childhood – if what he said was true – and was now dealing with the resulting anger issues, was trying to resolve them by wearing black and hanging off Dillon's every word. Since meeting Seth on her second night at the student bar, Eleanor had felt flattered by his unending attention, his constant acquiescing to her whims, the way his eyes followed her around every room. And he wasn't bad-looking, in a baby-faced kind of way. Although his new attempt at growing a beard looked ridiculous, not that she'd ever tell him that. But he wasn't enough of a challenge; conquering him had been too easy. And that wasn't satisfactory at all, there was no way Seth was ever going to stretch her to breaking point or to elevate her to the highest ecstasies. But she had a feeling that if she played her cards right, Dillon – self-proclaimed prophet of Satan – might just be the one to do that. And if becoming his follower meant she had easy access to this enigmatic man, then she was sure as hell going to every meeting. Granted, Satansim didn't interest her quite as much as Dillon did, but hey, who cared about that little detail? Seth hadn't seemed bothered by – or maybe hadn't even noticed – her regular little chats with Dillon during the meeting breaks, the way they stared at each other or the fact that they'd started texting each other. She'd deal with the fallout with her puppy dog later, when the inevitable time came. It was a small price to pay if it meant Dillon was going to be hers.

One of the other girls in her master's class – Ebony – had hinted that it would be wise to steer clear from Dillon, after she'd spotted Eleanor talking to him outside the canteen.

'I've heard he's bad news, Eleanor,' she'd said, her brow wrinkling. 'From what my friend was telling me, his past is quite twisted.'

All the better, Eleanor thought, rolling over and hugging her pillow. It was partly that darkness that attracted her to him. She was sick of always being the 'good girl', who lived up to her father's expectations. She wanted excitement, she wanted to plunge to the depths with Dillon as well as the heights. She planned to become immersed in his aura until they became symbiotic and inseparable. Ah, she was definitely a girl on a mission. She hugged herself, enjoying the thought.

Okay, so it was really important that she looked the part, she needed to appear impossibly ravishing. Turning to glance over at her wardrobe, she gazed at the sexy black outfit that was hanging over the mirror at the front. She'd been putting it together for days, tweaking it here and there, and had to admit it was looking pretty damn hot. Hopefully Dillon would think so too when he was looking at it on her. Or taking it off her...

Sitting up and swinging her legs over the side of the bed, Eleanor shivered, a wave of pleasure sweeping throughout her body. Tonight was the night she planned to make Dillon hers. And with the preparation she'd put into everything, what could possibly go wrong? Unaware that what was to come would be the last evening of her life, she stood up and sashayed over to her wardrobe...

$$3$$

Seth Hamilton ran down the stairs and opened the front door, slamming it loudly behind him. Listening to his mum and her arsehole boyfriend screaming at each other was doing his head in. It always did. He couldn't bear to be in that house for one minute longer.

'You were flashing your bloody eyes at Simon again,' Matt had shouted. 'You always do that when we go to the pub.'

'No I wasn't,' his mum had yelled back. 'You're fucking paranoid. It's the weed, you're smoking too much of it, Matt.'

'You're a slag, you are,' Matt had replied, his tone becoming threatening.

There was no way he was going home tonight, Seth decided, he'd stay at the university with someone – hopefully with Eleanor. But if she still had work to do, Hunter would take him in, he always did. Much to Natalie's annoyance.

Seth hated both of those people at home; he hated his mum for being weak and stupid enough to have such bad taste in men, and he hated that prick Matt even more for the way he treated his mum, always slagging her off and putting her down. It had always been like this at home. He couldn't even remember his dad leaving all those years ago, he'd been too young. Since his father had gone, a string of his mum's boyfriends had been in and out of the house and his life over the years, most of them bastards in some shape or form. Except Gary, but he'd left eventually, sick of his mum, Adele's mood swings. Seth had had enough of his mum and all. Oh God, how he wanted to leave home, set up in his own place. But he couldn't afford to right now. He wanted so much to better himself, forge out a different life to the shit one he'd been brought up in. University was the first step in doing that. Already in the second year of his BSC in computer science, he was pleased with how it was going. He was passing more assignments than he was failing. And he wasn't going to worry about paying back that big fuck-off student loan until the time came.

Anyway, he thought, rounding the corner out of the small council estate and kicking a traffic cone into the middle of the road, he'd met Eleanor now. He could really see a future with her. She was perfect in every way – she even smelled amazing. And she was so different from the tough, careworn girls he'd grown up with on the estate. There was just something about her. She was posh, but that didn't bother him. It turned him on in fact, the way she drawled some of her words, and wore expensive perfume, and knew how to charm anyone and everyone, from the tutors to the students, even Dillon. He hadn't been sure Eleanor would like the leader of New Satanism, he'd been worried that Dillon was too extreme for her. But he'd felt proud when she'd warmed to him and the group. She was such a lovely girl, she got on with everybody. So unlike his mum, who was edgy and paranoid, and hardly had any friends – those druggies she hung around with didn't count. As he imagined spending the night with Eleanor, Seth grinned for the first time in twenty-four hours.

They couldn't be more different, him and Eleanor, he

reflected, as he walked down the hill. From opposite ends of the social spectrum; him from a small house that still had holes in the walls from where one of his mum's boyfriends with an anger problem – Brett – had punched through the plaster whenever he'd had a drink. And he'd seen photos of Eleanor's home – God it was huge. With climbing plants and ivy round some of the many windows, it was like one of those dream houses he'd seen on the TV. It was in the country somewhere – had she said Sussex? Her dad owned twenty acres of land, she'd said, some of which he rented out to sheep farmers nowadays. Yes, that was the life Seth wanted; a bloody great house he would be proud to bring his friends back to, with grounds that stretched as far as he could see. It would have an enormous living room with an old-fashioned fireplace. He could see himself there now, sitting by the fire in the winter in a big leather chair, a hound or two at his feet. He sighed. But that all seemed a very long way off right now.

As he reached the bottom of Moreton Road, Seth turned right into Buckingham's high street. A mixture of shops trundled away before him on his right, and ancient Buckingham Old Gaol sat on his left – an unexpected fixture in the middle of the road. The narrow pavement was as busy as usual, with mums holding their kids' hands, and elderly couples walking their dogs. Most students in the university town wouldn't be up yet, he suspected. The streets belonged to them later in the day.

He rolled his tongue piercing around in his mouth, staring ahead without taking in much of the hustle and bustle around him, quickly becoming lost in deep thought. Tonight, he was going to tell Eleanor how he really felt about her. It was going to be hard, he knew that, he found opening up about his feelings difficult. He always had, he'd had to learn pretty quickly in life to keep his real self hidden, for protection reasons. His mum's boyfriends had often teased and taunted him mercilessly. But she was worth it, Eleanor was worth him digging deep and having the courage to open up. And he couldn't bear the thought of her ever finding someone else. That would make him so mad, it would destroy him. He kicked a bin, the imagined feelings of rejection too much to bear. Yes, he thought. He would do just about anything to keep Eleanor. One day, he was sure, she would help him get out of his shithole estate. They would be so happy together. Hopefully forever...

4

———

'Gloria...' Shirley was saying. 'Stop shouting for a minute. Gloria... just listen to me...'

Her sister had been yelling at her down the phone, barely pausing to draw breath, for over four minutes now. For the first half of this verbal blitz she'd felt bad, not liking to upset Gloria with the news that Noah was taking a break from his studies to work for her. Knowing she just had to bite the bullet and get the news over with, Shirley had simply blurted it out in her typical blunt fashion. And her sister had been just as upset as she'd predicted. But for the last two minutes Gloria's incessant voice – which was getting higher and more hysterical second by second – was pissing her right off. Her hangover was already making her feel like death warmed up and this onslaught really was the last thing she needed. She took a deep breath...

'GLORIA,' she shouted. 'SHUT THE FUCK UP FOR JUST ONE MINUTE AND LISTEN TO ME, WILL YOU?'

A stunned silence on the other end of the phone was the reply.

'Right,' Shirley said, clearing her throat. 'Now we might just have a chance of getting somewhere.'

'But...' Gloria said.

'Nope,' Shirley said quickly. 'It's my turn to speak now.' She sighed. 'Listen, Gloria. I really do understand how worried you are about Noah. He's incredibly clever, probably a bloody genius, but he's got the social skills of a dead gnat. You're probably – understandably – concerned that educating him to the highest degree is his only way forward in life, his greatest chance of success for the future. Because, let's face it, he's not going to get anywhere by networking and partying with the right crowd, is he? He doesn't even like most people.'

'I can hear what you're saying, you know,' Noah's voice called from the kitchen.

'Then stop bloody eavesdropping and get on with scrubbing those pans,' Shirley shouted back. 'You said you liked cleaning, so do some. Sorry, Gloria, where were we? Oh yes. So I do understand where you're coming from, you're his mum and you love him, and you're worried he's fucking his whole life up by leaving college.'

'You wouldn't understand, Shirl.' Gloria sniffed. 'You don't have any kids. You can't imagine...'

'No,' Shirley said. 'I don't have any children, but maybe that fact is helping me see this situation more clearly, without any maternal hormones getting in the way. Gloria, the thing is, by making Noah go to college, you're not actually listening to what *he* wants out of life. He's told you several times he doesn't want to go, but you're still making him. He's nearly a man now...'

'I'm eighteen in three months,' Noah called.

'Fuck off, Noah,' Shirley shouted. 'And stop listening. So, Gloria, you can't be in charge of his life forever. You need to trust him to make some of his own decisions. And if he wants to work with me, learn to be a private detective, well – at least it's a career choice, eh?'

Gloria let out a huge sob. Shirley rolled her eyes, waiting for the inevitable.

'But you haven't really got a career, have you, Shirl?' Gloria said, between hiccupping breaths. 'If we're honest about it? I mean, what work have you had this year? Hardly any.'

'I've had three cases so far this year, thank you very much, Gloria,' Shirley said, imagining a bottle of red wine together with a huge glass was floating towards her. 'I do all right for myself, I pay my bills with what I earn. And at least I've got a job.' She knew it was a cheap shot, but her pounding headache, and the fact that Noah wasn't supposed to be her problem in the first place, was making her tetchy.

'Shirley,' Gloria said with another sniff, sounding offended. 'You know I can't work because of my knees.'

'Yes, yes, all right,' Shirley said with a groan. 'Listen, you asked if Noah could come and stay with me, and I said yes because I wanted to help you out. He's been here for four months now and I've tried every way I can to make him go to college, but he really feels it's not for him at the moment. So maybe it's time to try something new for a change, for Noah to have a break from the normal routine. I've told him I'll give him three months as a trial, and if it doesn't work out he'll have to go back to college without a fuss, even if it means I have to staple his ears to the campus railings to get him to stay there.'

Gloria gave another sniff, but it was less loaded with tragedy than the previous ones.

'A trial?' she said, apparently not having taken it in the first time Shirley had tried to explain – which wasn't surprising given the decibels she'd instantly reached after hearing the words 'Noah's leaving college'. 'Okay, Shirl, maybe he does need a break from his studies for a bit.'

Shirley exhaled.

'Exactly, Gloria,' she said. 'You've got it, he does. And who knows, being my assistant may even work out for him.'

Her sister's snort indicated it was time to hang up before she became enraged to the point where she threw her phone across the room. The family had always been the same, always disparaging about Shirley's chosen career, making snide little remarks about it here and there. She'd been a bouncer back in the day, worked for a few pubs and clubs but mainly MK18's, the student hotspot, imaginatively named after Buckingham's postcode. She hadn't bothered with college or university, she liked to think she'd got her education from the school of life. Being a bouncer had given her prime opportunity to observe the pattern of human behaviour, as groups, couples and individuals went in and out. She'd watched and listened, and had started seeing patterns in their behaviour. Wanting more out of life, and after a particularly stressful night with two drunk lads who fancied themselves to be as hard as the Kray twins, the idea of becoming a private detective had suddenly come to her. Her mate Paul had done it; he'd left and become a copper. Shirley had fancied a different type of sleuthing work; her own business.

Finding out that in the UK a person didn't need any formal training for the role, she'd immersed herself in research and eventually set up as one. Never one to do things by halves, and discovering it was possible to become licenced in the role, Shirley had set about using her savings to attain the relevant qualifications: the IQ Level 3 Award and the fit-and-proper-person test, then she'd forked out for the licence fee. Not content to stop there, she'd taken online courses in surveillance, forensics and investigation and joined the Institute of Professional Investigators. Much to the ridicule of the family. It was annoying, because deep down she suspected they might be right, that maybe she didn't have it in her to be a really good private detective. Even her ex, Tiffany – who she was trying very hard not to think about – hadn't been all that interested in her line of work. Not that she could ever compete with Tiffany's high-flying career in sales. Shirley would never admit to being insecure about her business. But let's face it, it wasn't as though the phone was ringing off the hook, was it?

Quickly telling Gloria she needed to ring the college and sort it out, she said her goodbyes, rung off and chucked the phone on the now sparkling coffee table in front of her. Noah had already made a good start with cleaning up her previous night's mess, after she'd told him to leave her desk alone for a while. There was that one file she had in her possession that he could never see; that no one must ever see. She was pretty sure she'd hidden it safely away, but she wanted to check when he wasn't in the room, and before he started rooting around and tidying up. The material in that file was dangerous all right, and she needed to be sure no one ever, *ever* got even close to finding it.

5

Hunter McPherson slowly dug his cutting knife into the basswood, enjoying the twinge of excitement he always felt when starting a new piece. It was the way the wood smelt when he gently sliced it, and the way anything could be created from nothing – it was a process of creation. In front of him, at the back of the desk, stood an array of wooden figurines – all of them Norse gods and Vikings. His favourite was Odin of course. That one had come out beautifully. He'd wondered many times whether he'd ever be able to make another figure of that standard, so smooth, so perfect. Whittling was a kind of therapy for him, he reflected, slicing the wood with care. The fact that he'd learnt how to do it during his time in prison was something that Natalie and the others didn't need to know. Mind you, there was a lot they didn't need to know about Hunter's former life. And he was a changed person now. Well, mostly…

He breathed in the delicious icy air whooshing through his slightly opened window. He always had to have his windows open, even when it snowed. His need for this had happened since he'd got out of prison six years ago; he now felt trapped, claustrophobic, as if he was imprisoned in an airless room or a

29

car for too long. He'd spent so many years inside he was allergic to ever being confined again. And the plus side was he rarely felt the cold – he had too much padding for that. He grinned at the thought, allowing himself a brief flex of his enormous arm muscles.

The beautiful Eleanor was always whinging about the lack of heating in this place, but Hunter preferred it like that. Mind you, Eleanor was a posh rich kid who was used to her expensive centrally heated home. A brief frown flitted across his brow, as a pang of worry for little Seth affected him. That boy was besotted with Eleanor, but Hunter had been around the block a few times and could read the signs; that girl wasn't in love with him at all, the way she flirted with other men at the student bar. And he'd seen the way she'd looked at Dillon at the meeting last week. She'd break Seth's heart all right, then he – Hunter – would be there to help pick up the pieces. The one time he'd tried to bring it up with Seth hadn't gone well at all, the boy had got angry, his usual nought to one hundred temper coming into play. Hunter sighed. Ah well, he'd have to let nature take its course, he supposed. And be there with a comforting beer and spliff for Seth when it all went tits up. Not that Natalie would approve of that...

Hunter was really trying to be patient with Natalie, but he couldn't help wondering how long their relationship would last. She was so jealous, always accusing him of liking other women. Once upon a time, Hunter was that person who played the field, but not anymore. Although a boy could look without touching, couldn't he? They'd met in class, both studying for a bachelor's degree in Classical Studies. Natalie was cool, with her blue hair and piercings, and the understated way she took on life. His little pixie, he called her. But he sometimes wondered if Natalie could read his thoughts. Because although he never actually flirted with the girls at the university, or with anyone else for that matter, there was one that had piqued his interest.

Against his better judgement Hunter *did* find Eleanor attractive. He admitted to himself that most men probably did, when in her presence. There was something alluring about her free-spiritedness, the way she was bubbly and outgoing. And, of course, she was stunning, with a ridiculously hot body. Seth was a lucky man to have her, even though he was clearly riding for a fall. But she was irritating and high maintenance too. She'd never do as a long-term girlfriend, too much hard work. Hunter tried hard to push away the thought that he wouldn't mind having just one night with Eleanor. Just one. Because he knew it would probably be amazing...

No, he commanded his brain quickly. He must NOT think about Eleanor in that way. For the love of God, had he not learned his lesson last time, when he'd started fantasising about spending the night with that girl, after everything that had happened afterwards?

He shook his head, trying to release his thoughts, then stabbed the wood hard with the knife.

6

———

Shirley was trying to look interested as Noah pointed at his laptop. She'd downed four painkillers while chucking back a pint of water, and her headache was at last starting to recede. Noah had been as good as his word so far, clearly enjoying his new role in life, and had cleaned her kitchen to the degree that she now barely recognised it. After a lunch of sandwiches and crisps – put together by Noah – they were now sitting down to apparently discuss her website.

'What kind of online presence do you have in general, Shirley?' Noah was asking, as he peered at the screen. 'I mean, don't take this the wrong way, but your website's rubbish. No wonder it's not appealing to people. I mean, look at it – just one page of uninviting small print.'

'Online presence?' Shirley said, trying to heave herself forward. 'For God's sake, Noah. I've only just worked out how to use my bloody phone. I'm not exactly Bill Gates, am I? I don't have a fucking online presence. I have business cards, a telephone number, a few adverts on other sites and this website.'

'Ah.' Noah nodded wisely. 'I see. Well, that's your first mistake. Everything is done digitally now – people will be searching for reviews about you, and comparing your page with other private investigators' ones. We'll need a whole revamp; a new website – which I can set up, as well as a Twitter account and Facebook page. Oh, and I'll join you to Instagram and Pinterest too.'

'Urgh,' Shirley said with a sigh. 'All that does my head in if I'm honest with you, Noah. But if joining the modern world will mean boosting client enquiries, then by all means, knock yourself out.'

'Great,' Noah said, turning his serious face towards her enormous blotchy one. Which was now mascara free, after her half-hearted attempt to look human about an hour ago. She'd had a quick cry over Tiffany in the bathroom, allowed herself to feel the sting of her girlfriend leaving for a little while. Let the heavy pain of separation be acknowledged in her heart, permitted the knowledge of how much she bloody missed her to come to the forefront of her mind. She tried to tell herself that she and Tiffany were better off apart, that all the arguments they'd ended up having – sometimes on a daily basis – weren't healthy. Were damaging and destructive. Not that Noah ever seemed bothered by hearing them have a go at each other in the evenings, but then he tended to spend most of his time in his room. The problem was that she and Tiffany both liked having things their own way. They were both dominant in their views, strong personalities, and that was what had led to most of the conflict. Neither was prepared to back down and concede to the other. And deep down, she knew she was better off without that kind of negativity. But her heart still ached, though, damn it, she still bloody missed Tiffany, but right now she was going to ignore those feelings – or try to – and instead focus very hard on what Noah was saying.

'Another thing, Shirley,' her nephew went on. 'What do you call your practice? Have you got a name for it?'

'Yes, I call it my name, Shirley Butterworth, you plonker. What else would I call it?' Shirley said.

Noah shook his head.

'No,' he said. 'That's your second mistake, Shirley. You need a catchy name. A pithy one, something people will remember. Have a think about it.'

'Pithy?' Shirley said with a snort. 'Fuck off. How about "Give me your cash and I'll find out if your husband is cheating on you". Is that pithy enough?'

Noah stared at her without blinking.

'I don't think you're taking this seriously, Shirley,' he said. 'If I'm going to help you get more clients, I'm going to need you to work with me on this.'

Shirley looked at him. Blimey, how quickly roles could reverse, she thought. *This morning I was the adult, trying to get him to college. Albeit a still slightly drunk one. And now he's looking at me like a disappointed headmaster, and I feel like I'm going to be put in detention for messing around.*

'Fine,' she said with a cough. 'I'll think about a name. Happy?'

He nodded, and turned back to his laptop. As she gazed at him squinting at the screen, looking cheerier and more engaged than he'd done for months, a strange sensation occurred within her. It had something to do with the burden of worry about her business, that had occupied her mind for so long. What she'd said to Gloria earlier about her work paying her bills hadn't been entirely true. In fact, her credit rating was currently fucked as she'd missed so many payments. And the thought of losing her beloved house, even in the ramshackle state most of it was in – bar Noah's room – had started making her feel light-headed. Then when things had gone tits up with Tiffany, who'd been her partner for nearly a year, and lived with her for just over seven months, Shirley had started having what she reluctantly suspected were panic attacks. Dreading an argument with Tiffany every day, after their relationship had started to sour, and hiding the bills from energy companies at the back of her desk, she'd suddenly become overwhelmed with a feeling of doom, and her breathing would become shallow, her heart rate faster. She'd have to sit down, the room feeling odd and unfamiliar around her, and the harder she tried to make the stress go away, the more forcefully it pushed back and refused to. She never discussed this with anyone, definitely not Noah, the little twerp, and Tiffany had dismissed it, telling her that there were a lot of people worse off in life than her and that she should just ignore the feelings, go out for a walk or something. Hah, like that ever worked. And after all, she had her hard image to maintain with Noah. Losing that would be the final stamp of defeat. But inside she'd known she was losing her marbles to anxiety. The bloody thing had taken over her brain.

But now, looking at Noah tapping away on his laptop so industriously, that feeling – the horrible brace of worry – was lifting, just a tiny bit. An incremental easing of a cortisol-flooded habit. A teeny-tiny ray of hope – that things with her business might actually get off the ground now – crept in. *Crikey*, she thought. *Noah's doing a good job with this. Maybe, just maybe, this him working with me thing might actually work out...*

7

Natalie Sadler layered another thick line of black kohl across her left eyelid. She stepped back and surveyed her work in the mirror. Yes, she thought. That would do. She looked all right. Suddenly, an image of what Eleanor would probably look like that evening flashed through her mind, and her skinny shoulders drooped. She could see Eleanor sashaying in to the ruined temple, smiling, her tight black clothes showing off her curvy figure. All the men in the room would look at her with lust. They always did, even Hunter, although he'd tried to hide it from her. And some of the girls would too, or with thinly disguised envy. Jesus, why did her mind torture her like this? Natalie wondered, aware of the sinking feeling in her stomach. It was constantly comparing her to that spoilt lucky girl, who had bloody everything in life going for her. She gazed at the small brown eyes looking back at her in the mirror. They were now largely disguised with an hour's worth of make-up application. God, she thought. I actually look like a freak. Why do I bother putting the effort in?

Her mother's voice went round in her head. 'You'll never be pretty, Natalie,' she'd said once. 'You're a plain duckling, just like me.' But then her mother hardly ever said anything encouraging to her. It wasn't that her mum's little digs were outright rude, it was just that they were relentless, and had built up and up over the years, eroding Natalie's self-esteem; dimming her view of herself, making her try to become small in every sense, to hide herself away. 'Why are you wearing that, it doesn't suit you?' 'You've got your father's chin, such a shame.' Every comment wore away a tiny bit of Natalie's inner light, she could feel it happening, it was almost a physical sensation. And for some reason she never had the inner resources to stoke the light up and make it shine brighter again.

And then at uni she'd got together with Hunter, and she'd been *so* happy, at least to start with. He was everything she'd ever wanted, and more. A beautiful person on the inside and out, with muscles to die for. He was someone to look up to, a positive force in her life. And he seemed to like her exactly the way she was, always boosting her confidence with supportive remarks and observations. Always complimenting what she wore, or how she looked. She'd never had a serious boyfriend before, not for more than a couple of weeks, so being with Hunter had felt like an achievement, she suddenly felt like a *someone* in life – a girl who was worthy of having a gorgeous boyfriend. When she was with Hunter, she didn't mind people looking at her, noticing her.

But then Seth had got with Eleanor, and that girl had changed everything. Natalie could feel herself becoming quieter and more awkward whenever Eleanor was around. The problem was that she felt so overshadowed by Eleanor's easy manner and confidence, her stunning looks, and the way she didn't seem to have to make an effort to enjoy life. Natalie always felt like a dowdy freak next to her; suddenly her blue hair, that she had originally thought looked so cool, seemed stupid and immature. Her mousey face felt like it was shrinking, pinching together, the more she looked at Eleanor's open one. Her heart twisted into knots every time Eleanor even spoke to Hunter, and he replied. Of course, he must find Eleanor attractive. Because she was, she was more than that, she was God damn beautiful and sexy. And she showed up everything that Natalie knew she wasn't.

Suddenly hanging out with her friends felt like a nightmare, Natalie no longer enjoyed their company so much, and dreaded any event that she knew Eleanor would attend, especially the New Satanism Society. Which was a shame as she hadn't had many friends at school, and had felt really proud of the friendships she'd forged at university. She'd decided to try and make Hunter stay in with her more in the evenings, watching films and having dinner together. She'd even suggested they could have a break from New Satanism for a while, and that maybe he could teach her to play games on the PlayStation.

'Come on, baby, it will be nice,' she'd said. 'Just you and me, and I'll cook your favourite dinner...'

But it was as though he could read her mind, knew where she was going with this. He'd nicely but firmly explained that he needed his social life to keep on track in order for him to feel happy. And that he had no plans at all to stop seeing his friends. He said he loved being with her, and that they *did* do things together – just the two of them – sometimes. But that it was important for them to be healthy socially too. Hunter always talked like that; sometimes he seemed even older than his thirty-one years. And that was another thing, she felt so young and inexperienced next to him. She worried she wasn't exciting enough for him, or perhaps worldly enough. She didn't like the fact that he smoked cannabis, to be honest she hated him doing anything that took his attention away from her. Even that bloody whittling was annoying. He was doing it more and more these days...

Natalie's head drooped and she turned, walking across the

room, then swinging round to pace back again. She hardly even noticed that she was wringing her hands. Her world felt like it was changing, and she felt powerless to do anything about it. She had the sense that she was just an insignificant atom in the universe that was slowly being eroded away by forces greater than her. Oh, why did Eleanor have to come in to their lives? And why wasn't there anything she could do to change things?

8

———

Dillon Rushwell checked his phone. 7.50pm. His followers would start arriving any minute now. The temple was ready; he'd already drawn on the chalk pentagons and lit the candles; now the archaic space abounded with dark shadows, bouncing in the freezing breeze that crept through old cracks. The altar – shrouded in black as usual – held the important objects of ritual, which would be used in due course.

He always arrived early to set things up, he knew his creation of the perfect atmosphere lay in forward planning. Most of it was just for show, to set the scene for the members so that they could really get into it and feel the power inside themselves, and in case any university staff ever 'popped in' to see what was going on. 'Just dramatic play,' he'd explain. 'Just a bit of fun and theatricality. It's an important function for our progressive group, it's how we explore our beliefs.' The really important message came in the words Dillon said to the group, in the control and command he exerted over them through language, sometimes subtly, at other times boldly. His followers were now starting to get his message, he could see that: that he *was* Satan's prophet, that he received messages from the eternal rebel that they needed to listen to and adhere to. And they liked it, they wanted more of it. A rush of adrenaline shivered down his spine.

Dillon opened his black bag and took out his mirror, checking his eyes. Still looking good, he thought, superbly outlined with black eyeliner, which made them appear even more intense and sparkling. It was important that he looked the part at all times. He'd noticed some of the boys in the group had started copying his use of eyeliner – which was fantastic, as he knew it meant they really admired him. Yet another sign of how much he could influence those near him, putting them under his spell whenever it took his fancy.

Dillon had first noticed he could wield a strange power over the people around him at an early age. He must have been around twelve when he'd started enjoying his gift properly, shaping and changing any social situation he found himself in. Since then, loads of girls had told him he was 'magnetic', and boys seemed drawn to him, wanted to be like him. From the loyalty his followers showed him now, he suspected there was something magnetic and addictive about him. Of course, he wasn't everyone's cup of tea, the more conservative people he met tended to fear him, actively avoid him. But for many, he became an idol. Life really couldn't be better.

Snapping the mirror back together, he placed it carefully into his meticulously arranged bag. Everything about Dillon's life was meticulously arranged, from his wardrobe, to his personal belongings, to his thoughts. He'd often wondered if everyone's brain worked like his; reading people, events and circumstances with incisive, fast precision, then being able to manipulate – actually he thought of it as 'create' – the best way forward for himself in any given circumstances. It was as though life was a game, and he was the grand chess master. Always one step ahead, always laughing in his mind with the enjoyment of it all.

He looked down at his body with admiration, something he liked to do several times a day. Fuck, if he was a girl, he would fancy himself, he thought. But then he deserved the streamlined muscles he had, he constantly put the work in to maintain them, sticking to a strict running and weights schedule. Checking out the latest ink work on his arm, he concluded that the tattoo artist had done a great job – although it had been hard to find space for it. They'd decided on a bare patch near his shoulder in the end. The design was yet another version of the Sigil of Baphomet, the official insignia of Satan followers. Well, to be accurate, it was the sign for members of the Church of Satan, which Dillon's group was loosely based on, as it was with the practices of the Satanic Temple. The New Satanism Society was actually a far more accurate interpretation of Satanic culture in his opinion, than either of the two main Satanic belief systems currently in existence. His was one fine-tuned by Dillon himself; he'd named it. And it differed from the Church of Satan and the Satanic Temple's beliefs too; New Satanism wasn't just about using the name Satan to symbolise the 'eternal rebel', as the Satanic Temple said it was. The Satanic Temple's followers rejected the belief in the supernatural. And the Church of Satan described themselves as atheists who use Satan as a symbol of 'pride, liberty and individualism'. Whereas Dillon knew that the Devil was real, and was in him, he could feel Him there, guiding him. Which was so very exciting...

Craning his neck a bit, he could see the tattoo was looking good, still a bit red in places but that would settle down over the next day or two. It still hurt, he smarted, but he enjoyed the pain. It turned him on. Because, after all, life was about the successful incorporation of dark and pain, with the light. And not many people knew that, they were too busy being sheep, following the socially conditioned herd, baaing and bleating, and wanting to be told what to do and think, acting as though they were fine, when really – on the inside – they were lost and in denial. Dillon enjoyed the dark, as well as the light. It was the only way to feel truly alive, and to understand who he was, and what his life was about. And nothing gave him greater happiness and pleasure than to see other people doing the same.

Eleanor was hot, he was glad she'd joined his group. Now there was a girl who could be moulded into the ideal Dillon follower. He had, in fact, spotted her around university long before she'd known who he was; watched her, as he'd mended a door, cleaned a window, fixed a pipe. What she didn't know was that *she* was *his* target, not the other way around, as she so obviously thought. When he saw something he wanted, he knew immediately. And always got it in the end. Eleanor interested him, she had an air of intrigue about her, and she was by far the most beautiful girl in his society, different from his usual female followers; the way her blonde hair cascaded over her shoulders, her cherry red lips broke into that ravishing smile. Her blue eyes spoke to him, it seemed. He could read them as he could read her heart. She was confident, always a bonus, and seemed comfortable in the group. Her attention made him feel good; Dillon thrived on admiration and devotion, it made him feel really alive and glowing. Some part of him was aware that he needed it constantly, like a junkie needed drugs. If he didn't have it, now that's when problems arose. Things got very ugly and dark then, often violent. But he never gave much thought to that detail, because he really didn't care what it meant about him psychologically. And most of his past secrets had been stowed far away from everyone anyway, no need to worry about them now that he was revered and adored... And Eleanor looked like she was ready to give him admiration and devotion in bucketloads. She was literally gagging for him, bless her... But he would continue to carefully and consciously play the game, not appear too overenthusiastic to start with. After all, it was important that he carried on reeling her in, making her want more, until she felt absolutely ready to burst. Dillon loved this part of the process, gaining power over another person; it was the ultimate intoxication.

Ah, the door was opening; that old piece of work always squeaked like a rodent whenever anyone went in or out. The first of his followers must be arriving. He stood up straight, rolling his shoulders back. Let the fun begin, he thought with a grin.

'Come to us, Satan,' Dillon said loudly...

9

———

Shirley shook her pillow with vigour until the lumps and bumps in it dispersed. Blimey, she thought, lying down. What a day could bring. Noah had surpassed himself, she had to give the kid that. By the time she'd finally given in to the remnants of her hangover at 9.30pm and trudged upstairs, the boy had already set her up a flashy new website. *And* he'd given her practice a new name. He'd called the process rebranding, and she'd had a chuckle about that – mainly because he was using such a knobby buzzword, and anyway, there wasn't much there to rebrand in the first place. His efforts had definitely distracted her from her internal moping about Tiffany's departure too. Not that it didn't still hurt – it did. Hurt like fuck, in fact. But she currently had something new to concentrate on...

Now, if any potential client cared to click on one of the many links to her site that Noah had apparently scattered throughout the virtual web, they would be greeted with the name: Justice Investigations. She'd had to admit it was good, well, better than boring old Shirley Butterworth anyway. Noah had first suggested Probing Investigations, but she'd quickly vetoed that one, stating loudly that she wasn't running a frigging colonoscopy practice.

As her heavy eyelids closed, Shirley thought how wonderful it would be if all Noah's messing around on the web actually worked. What if she received a phone call from a potential client the next day? *Nah, don't be daft, Shirl,* she quickly reprimanded herself with a small smile. *You can dream, but don't be silly about it, because you'll just feel let down when it doesn't pan out...*

10

———————

Eleanor wiped the faint layer of sweat from her forehead, the freezing temperature outside forgotten. She pulled her phone from her black bag and looked down: it was 10.05pm. Their weekly New Satanism session had just come to an end. The last two hours had been what they always were in the ruined temple; the time had whizzed by in a blur of shadows, fire, excitement, music and role play, and most importantly Dillon being Dillon. He'd put a black mask on at one point, but she had still seen his sexy eyes peering through it, often at her. They should all get themselves masks, he'd said. He wanted to see as many people as possible wearing them next week; the more creative the better, he wanted to see skulls, demons, dogs, Baphomet – the goat head that Dillon said symbolised the reconciliation of opposites, whatever. Masks are symbolic, he'd said. Eleanor was worried how her make-up would hold up under one, there was no way she wanted her face to look all sweaty at the end of a session.

They'd worshipped Satan, made Devil horns with their hands, and chanted the New Satanism tenets, which was basically about being free and having the freedom to do anything, as long as it didn't violate anyone else, and being blasphemous as it challenged the ignorant religions that held power over the world. And how they had to follow the wisdom of their Grand Master, Dillon. He'd given a passionate speech about how embracing Satanism meant embracing personal liberty and personal independence. He'd then poked fun at the sceptics who believed that all Satanists did was sacrifice kids on altars. This was greeted with roars and laughs from around the room. Dillon's followers had hung on his every word throughout the whole session, she'd noticed, lapping up his wisdom. She'd wondered what it was like to have that kind of power. He'd performed a black mass from behind the altar that he said was an expression of freedom to be different, to be themselves. They'd put on the cloaks he'd brought, and amid the eerie shadows, candles, chalked-on inverted pentagrams, body heat and movement, the temple had really warmed up. Near the end, Dillon had said they were each going to perform an annihilation ritual next week; although she wasn't clear what that actually was.

Eleanor had arrived at the temple later than planned, and this had thrown her off track. She'd planned to make an early arrival, wanting to sufficiently dazzle Dillon with her outfit; intending to make sure he had time to take it in before he was distracted by too many of the others. But Daniel had rung just as she was leaving the halls, wanting to discuss the diabolical state of the essay she'd sent off last night. Typical Daniel, always so keen to pull his students straight up on any detail that annoyed him. She'd eventually placated him with promises to rewrite the piece, but by the time she'd got to the tumbledown building, stumbling up the old path in the dark, with the freezing wind slashing her hair to and fro, the session had already started.

Eleanor had spotted, during her first time at the temple, that most of Dillon's followers were outcasts in some way; people who felt themselves to be outsiders, who normally had trouble feeling like they belonged in any group. But in this group, being an outsider was actually celebrated and encouraged. She wasn't stupid, she knew a lot of people thought she had an easy life, and would never in a million years have considered her a social misfit of any sort. But that's because they didn't know who she was on the inside, didn't know how emotionally dependent her adoptive father had always been on her, living vicariously through his pretty daughter; wanting and needing her to be perfect in every way so he could continue his idolisation of her, still present even now that he was confined to a wheelchair. Growing up, she'd always made choices that would please him, dressed in a way he was proud of, and eventually she'd realised she didn't know who she – Eleanor – was at all. Because she was her father's creation, she lived to please him, and be praised by him. On the odd occasion that she did something outside his remit, like when she'd decided to have her nose pierced when she was seventeen, he withdrew his love momentarily, acted disgusted and disappointed. So she'd taken the stud out again, of course she had. The thought of losing his approval had been too much to bear.

But now, away at university, she had freedom at last, she could explore anything she wanted and he'd never know, because when she went home she reverted back to how *he* wanted her to be. Eleanor felt like a chameleon, changing herself for different situations. The only problem was that she wasn't sure at all who she really was, her sense of identity was very fluid and weak. So yes, she did feel like an outsider, especially when she was surrounded by all these students with strong personalities. Oh, she could act as though she had one too, but that's exactly what it was, an act.

She gazed over at the man who she loved, Dillon, who was chatting and laughing with Seth and Hunter by the door, while the rest of the throng pushed past them in dribs and drabs, wrapping their coats around themselves in preparation for the November night's air. Strange little Natalie, as always, was standing a few feet away, staring at Hunter. Dillon towered over the other three, his long hair wound up on his head making him so elegant; he was at least a foot taller than Seth and several inches higher than Hunter. Natalie looked even tinier than usual. Eleanor watched Dillon's muscles, slender but strong – his tattoos adorning them. Now, Dillon was the person who would help her find herself, she was sure of it. The way he talked, he seemed so sorted, so *himself*. He would know how to bring the real Eleanor out. And then she would feel whole, fully formed. Dillon's eyes looked away from Seth's, and found hers. An electric bolt ran straight through her body. But she made sure she didn't drop her gaze. He beckoned her to join them.

Seth put his arm round her waist as Eleanor arrived beside him, squeezing her towards him, his eyes hungrily seeking out her own. She tried not to tense up, didn't want to make him feel bad. He'd put black make-up round his eyes like Dillon. For a minute a pang of guilt thrashed through her, as she realised how devastated Seth would be when he knew it was over, at least sexually between them.

'Hi, baby,' he said, beads of sweat still on his forehead. 'It was good tonight, wasn't it?'

'Oh yes,' she said, glancing at Dillon. 'It always is.' Oh God, he was divine. His hair, his eyes, his bare arms, everything about him was...

Dillon's eyes crinkled at the edges and the corners of his lips turned up just a fraction.

'I aim to please,' he said in his husky voice. 'Glad you enjoyed it. Don't forget about the annihilation ritual next week – it's important you all bring an object that symbolises some sort of pain that has been put on you in your life. What we'll do will get rid of that hurt forever.' There was something mischievous about his smile.

'Actually, I was going to ask you about that,' Eleanor said, turning fully towards him. Could this be her chance to get him on his own? 'Could you tell me more about it? I'm not sure I really understand yet.'

'No problem,' Dillon said. 'Why don't you stay behind and help me clear away these candles and cloaks, and I'll tell you everything you want to know.'

As she turned back she saw Seth's expression freeze.

'But I thought we were going to the student bar for some drinks?' he said, his body going rigid next to hers. 'I texted you about it earlier, Ellie, and you said it was a good idea?'

'I'll meet you there soon,' Eleanor said, trying to make her voice soothing, leaning forward to give Seth a kiss on the cheek before flashing him her best smile. God, she felt like a bitch now, but she couldn't help it. Her feelings for Dillon were too strong, it was like a more powerful force than her own will had taken her over. 'I won't be long, I promise. I'm new to all this, remember, and there's a lot about New Satanism that I still don't know. You guys have been coming to meetings for much longer than me. Go on, and I'll meet you at the bar in a little while.'

Ignoring Seth's pleading eyes, and the fact that Hunter was shaking his head ever so slightly, she turned back to Dillon.

'Thanks,' she said. 'What do I put the candles in?'

'There's a black sack by the wall over there.' Dillon motioned to the back of the temple. He held her gaze for a second longer than necessary. 'I'll come and enlighten you about the benefits of the annihilation ritual in just a second.'

He held the door wide, grinning as the other three – the last of the evening's revellers aside himself and Eleanor, Hunter, Natalie and Seth – trooped out.

'Don't worry.' Dillon winked at Seth. 'I'll take good care of her, she'll be back with you before you know it.'

Seth was still staring back, his expression unreadable, as Dillon closed the door in his face.

~

Ten hours later...

11

It was Doctor Abigail Dahiru who found the body the next morning. Late for the early faculty meeting, she walked quickly through the biting air, pulling her scarf tightly round her neck, inwardly groaning as she realised she'd left her glasses and her notepad at home again. At least she'd remembered her laptop and phone this time. Walking up the straight path towards the old mansion, the rolling grounds on either side of her covered in a layer of white frost, she wondered – not for the first time – why the damn car park had to be so far from the actual building.

Something to her right caught her eye, and she glanced over, not breaking her stride. Was that a pile of clothes lying there in the pond? Maybe one of the students had dropped them last night in the dark after going to the laundry room. Probably drunk as usual. No, it wasn't a pile of clothes, she determined, squinting at whatever it was. She better go and see. Bloody hell, this was going to make her even later, and Van Bern – who always chaired the meetings – had already made it known that he disapproved of her habitual tardiness. It wasn't her fault that the kids demanded so much attention in the mornings, was it?

She wasn't exactly superwoman, much as she tried to be sometimes. Swerving off the path and on to the grass, the frost crunched beneath her feet as she passed the decorative stone wall and accompanying classical figurines. As she neared the shallow pond, her hand went to her mouth and she stopped. It was a person lying there. A girl. From the icy blue of her skin she was almost definitely dead. Abigail let out a whimpering sound.

Bending down closer, she could see from the side of the face that it was that pretty girl, who was in Daniel's master's class. Was Eleanor her name? The girl's eye that she could see was open, staring. The rest of her head and half the girl's body was immersed in the pond, the rest of her body lay stiff on the freezing ground. Fighting the urge to vomit, Abigail stood up straight, dizziness rushing through her head. She fumbled in her bag, retrieving her phone. Help. She must get help straight away. Oh God, why was this happening? She punched in the numbers, her fingers trembling...

12

Shirley splashed water on her face, then dried it roughly with her towel. Bloody hell, she'd slept too long, it was nearly midday. Not very professional of her, was it? And she'd been hoping to sort her desk out, check she'd properly hidden the file that no one should ever see, before Noah woke up.

'Morning,' Noah said, as she stomped downstairs. 'Actually, it's nearly the afternoon.'

'I know, why the hell didn't you wake me up?' Shirley said with a growl. 'I've slept away half the goddam day.'

'You were so hung over yesterday, I thought you could do with the rest,' Noah said. 'Anyway,' he went on quickly, as Shirley opened her mouth to protest. 'You'll be glad to hear you've already had an enquiry from someone who saw your business on a Google ad I started for you yesterday. You left your phone down here when you went to bed last night, so I answered it for you.'

'Oh yeah?' Shirley felt a twinge of euphoria. 'Who's that then? What did they say?' *Blimey*, she thought. *This internet stuff works quickly, doesn't it?*

'She said her name's Katherine Mace.' Noah picked up the

writing pad next to him. 'She wants her ex-husband investigated for child support evasion.'

'Okay,' Shirley said slowly. 'That's a good start. Thanks, Noah.' Still, she couldn't help feeling just a tiny bit disappointed. A small part of her had been hoping for a really juicy case she could get her teeth into...

'So shall I phone her back and tell her you'll take her on?' Noah said, looking up at his aunt. 'Look, I went out this morning and got you a new diary for appointments, so you can stay as organised as possible.'

Shirley looked at the big black organiser he was brandishing at her.

'Great,' she said. 'Yes, tell her I'll have a chat with her. Maybe book her a time for a phone call tomorrow.'

'What about later today?' Noah raised his eyebrows. 'You might as well strike while the iron's hot, Shirley.'

'Fine,' Shirley said with a sigh. 'For later this afternoon then.' It was all very bloody well, Noah organising her so much, she thought. But she couldn't help feeling things were slightly being taken out of her hands. But then, she mused, maybe that's exactly what she needed. A kick up the arse. Even if it was from an annoying, socially dysfunctional seventeen-year-old. And she'd even got a potential client who'd enquired. Albeit about a not terribly exciting job, but still, beggars can't be choosers, she thought. Now, how could she get Noah to bugger off for a bit so she could check that file...

'Listen, clever clogs,' she said. 'Since you're doing such a good job with the tidying, I'm going to give you some money and I want you to walk into town and buy me a new writing pad, three files and a Dictaphone. They should sell all that at the stationer's. I want to make sure I'm ready if we get more cases coming in. Take your time when you're out, no rush. All right?'

'Yes,' Noah said, jumping out of the armchair. 'Anything else?'

'No, that should do for now,' Shirley said, sinking into the chair he'd warmed up for her. 'Bring me my handbag, and I'll give you the dosh.'

As the front door closed a few minutes later, Shirley looked over at her desk, torn between immediately checking the file was suitably hidden and making herself a strong coffee with three sugars.

Her phone, still on the arm of the chair where Noah had left it, bleeped into life, the *Star Wars* ringtone filling the air.

'Yeah?' she said, answering it. 'I mean, Justice Investigations, can I help you?'

'Is that Shirley Butterworth?' a man's voice said. It had a cracked quality to it, like old parchment.

'Yes, that's me,' Shirley said.

The man sighed.

'Good,' he said. 'I found you online. I want you to investigate the death of my daughter.'

13

———

Doctor Abigail Dahiru was still shaking. It had been the worst morning of her life, and the day wasn't over yet. After phoning the head of faculty, Eric Van Bern, while she was standing by the pond next to Eleanor's body, the next few hours had turned into a whirl of police cars and ambulances. Of course, the police – detectives actually, who'd introduced themselves as DI Linford and DS Ricci – had wanted to talk to her, and she'd answered all their questions as best she could, while feeling like she was having an out-of-body experience. The whole thing was so bizarre. Students just didn't drop down dead at the Royal Buckingham University. There would be an autopsy, they'd said. But the death didn't look suspicious. Poor Eleanor seemed to have been stumbling back to her room last night, after attending a club somewhere in the grounds, and lost her way in the dark. The police thought it looked like she'd fallen and hit her head, losing consciousness, and ending up in the pond where she'd probably drowned. But like all deaths that were unexpected, a post-mortem would be performed that afternoon, just to make sure.

'Thanks,' she said, as Daniel placed a steaming mug of tea in front of her. 'This is all a bloody nightmare, isn't it?'

'Yes.' He sighed. 'Poor Eleanor.'

They were in the staffroom. Abigail hadn't been able to eat any lunch. Flashbacks of Eleanor's body kept tormenting her mind. The eye, the stiffness of the body, the way the poor girl had just lain there, undetected, half in the pond. Probably for hours. Christ, if anything like that happened to any of her children... Two detectives were still chatting to Eric at the other end of the room. Abigail stared over at him. Their head of faculty had tears running down his jowly cheeks.

'Don't you think that's a bit odd?' she said, turning to Daniel, who had arranged himself in a nearby chair. 'Why is Eric so upset? He didn't really even know the girl, did he?'

Daniel shook his head.

'He's been acting strangely all day,' he said. 'But then old Eric is always a bit peculiar. I usually put it down to the fact that us academics tend to have an eccentric gene.'

'Speak for yourself,' Abigail said, a faint smile crossing her lips. 'But I know what you mean. I've just never seen Eric like this before.'

'No,' Daniel said, watching the man run his hands through what little hair he had left. 'But this is an awful business. I suppose you can never tell how you'll react until something like this happens. And you go around hoping it never does.'

'Quite,' Abigail said, her heart weighing heavily in her chest. 'She was so still, just lying there when I found her. So alone. What an awful way to go. And she was young and beautiful, with her whole life ahead of her. I know people always say things like that, but it's true.'

'Yes,' Daniel said. 'She was a good student. With the exception of her last essay.'

'Coming from you that's high praise indeed.' Abigail nodded, willing her hands to stop trembling enough for her to pick up her mug. 'She must have been bright then. What a waste.'

They watched Eric turn towards them as the detectives filed out of the staffroom.

'Such a tragedy,' he said, approaching them, his hands gesticulating wildly. Abigail could see that the man was shaking more than she was. 'I can't believe it. That it could happen. Why her? And on university grounds too. It must have been an accident, surely an accident. It's too awful, too awful.' He staggered off towards the sink.

Daniel frowned, as he watched his head of faculty go past.

14

Shirley put her phone down. Her head felt dazed. Wow, that had been unexpected. A Mr Alistair Parkhurst phoning, wanting her to investigate the death of his daughter at Royal Buckingham University. The police, he'd said, had already told him it didn't look suspicious. That they believed Eleanor, his daughter, had simply stumbled when going back to her room after attending some meeting last night, tripped, hit her head and ended up in a pond. He said an autopsy would be done that afternoon, but that he wanted to engage Shirley's services anyway. That he *knew* – and here the old boy's voice had become choked up – that Eleanor was far too smart to ever trip and fall into a pond. Something much more sinister had happened to her, he said. He could feel it, he'd known as soon as the policewoman had arrived at his house to tell him about Eleanor. Darker forces were at work here, mark his words, he'd said. He wanted the whole thing investigated from start to finish, by someone other than the police. Then he'd mentioned such an exorbitant sum that Shirley had nearly dropped her phone. He would be happy to pay her that, he'd said, if Justice Investigations could provide him with the answers he needed.

Eleanor was his only child, he'd explained. And his world was now completely shattered and would never be whole again. He was confined to a wheelchair, he wouldn't be able to go and make his own inquiries on the campus. And the last gift he could give his beloved daughter would be to find out exactly how she'd died, so she would be able to rest in peace.

Shirley stared straight ahead as she thought about all this, as a shaft of dim sunlight made its way through her grimy living-room window. Of course she'd said yes, agreed to take him on as a client. Quite apart from the money, which frankly she needed like a fish needed water, she'd been touched by the emotion in the old boy's voice. Had found herself really wanting to help him. But now the customary anxiety was rearing its ugly head. *What if you're not good enough to solve this case?* it whispered to her. *You should have told him to find a more experienced private detective. One that could actually help him.*

'Shut up,' she said out loud. Fuck, wasn't talking to yourself the first sign of madness?

'What was that?' Noah's voice called, as he let himself back in. 'Did you say something?'

'No, just coughed,' Shirley said. There was no way she'd tell him about her doubts. She had to appear confident at all costs. 'Come in and sit down, Noah. You're going to need to phone that Katherine Mace woman back and tell her I can't take her on at the moment. We've got a new case...'

15

S eth paused, taking a wild minute to survey the wreckage of
his bedroom. In just under two minutes, he'd obliterated
almost all of his possessions: his posters now lay torn and
trampled on the floor, his lamp was now smashed junk, his
wooden curtain pole had been ripped from the wall and broken
in half, multiple pages had been torn from books, and all the
items from his shelves lay scattered among the debris, most of
them now smashed and unusable. It was a good thing his mum
and her prick of a boyfriend Matt were out – probably at Matt's
dealer's flat – or they would be up here screaming at him to stop.
But Seth couldn't stop, he couldn't calm down, the incandescent
hurt and rage in him still screamed too loudly. Eleanor was
dead. DEAD. He aimed a kick at the door and heard the crack as
his foot went through it. Probably fractured a bone too, if the
resulting searing pain was anything to go by. But he didn't care.
He didn't care about anything at all now.

He picked up his careworn duvet – that hadn't had a cover on
it for over a year – and threw it on top of the remains of his
possessions on the carpet. Then he pulled his mattress off the
bedframe, opened the door and threw the lumpy piece of shit

out into the hall. Then he pulled his old rucksack out from between the old wooden slats, took his phone and wallet from his pockets and stuffed them into it, along with some underwear, a change of clothes and his phone charger. He didn't know where he was going, and it didn't really matter. He knew he just had to get away.

Because after what he'd done last night, his heart was telling him that Eleanor's death was probably his fault.

16

I t was Thursday afternoon, and Detective Inspector Charles Linford was reading through Eleanor Parkhurst's autopsy report. It had come back surprisingly quickly, he thought.

'Just as we suspected,' he said, turning to his colleague, Detective Sergeant Gabrielle Ricci. 'The university girl's death has been ruled accidental. Take a look while I go and brief the others.' He passed her the paper.

DS Ricci leant back against her desk, her eyes skimming down to the crucial paragraph of information.

> …In summary, it is my opinion that the main factor involved in bringing about the death of Eleanor Sabine Parkhurst was accidental drowning, as indicated by the large amount of froth present around the nostrils and in the upper and lower airways. Minor head trauma was also recorded, and is consistent with the female unintentionally falling and hitting her head on the large stone

(taken from the site and also examined) due to the weather conditions of that night. The accidental drowning occurred after an unintentional fall and possible loss of consciousness, as indicated by the small amount of haemorrhage in the region of the right forehead and in the nasion region. Alcohol is considered a contributing factor, as indicated by the high amounts of ethanol found in the blood.

Mode of death: accidental

No foul play suspected

Manner of death: accidental drowning

Time of death estimated between 11pm and 4am.

Well, DS Ricci thought, looking up. *That's that then. A very fast turnaround. Would the same conclusion have been so quickly reached if Thames Valley Police hadn't recently been criticised for rising crime rates in the area?* She understood the pressure on the force, of course she did. Crime in Buckingham had gone mad over the last year; reports of stabbings, thefts and drunken violence were at unprecedentedly high levels. Detective Chief Superintendent Paterson had left herself and her colleagues in no doubt that these levels needed to be lowered. ASAP, he'd said. But she hadn't thought Eleanor's cause of death would be determined quite so quickly. *Ah well*, she thought, *the coroner is a smart woman, she knows what she's talking about. So that just leaves me with the job of informing the father.* Speaking with relatives who'd just lost a loved one was never something she looked forward to, but after seventeen years in the job she knew how important it was to pass on relevant information to the families, and was good at disclosing it with appropriate amounts of compassion.

Standing up, she turned and chucked the report on to her desk. She'd phone Mr Parkhurst just as soon as she'd grabbed herself a coffee...

17

'Come on, Noah, get your arse in gear,' Shirley shouted. 'I've had Mr Parkhurst on the phone and he's furious, says the autopsy came back with accidental drowning. He's already emailed me the report. I'm going to study it properly this evening, but I had a quick look and what I saw has already made me question the verdict of accidental. Namely, the marks on her head and the haemorrhage in her forehead. A simple unintended trip over shouldn't cause that much damage, I'm going to get someone else to take a look at that, I need a second opinion.' She thought back to her forensics course; the tutor had specifically said that the diagnosis of drowning should only be made after the *exclusion* of other causes. Shirley wasn't convinced those other possible causes had been sufficiently looked at, the whole thing had been wrapped up so quickly. 'We need to get to the university pronto, look at the scene where Eleanor's body was found, and start interviewing. I've phoned the head honcho, the chancellor Professor Indigo Fielding, and told her we'll be coming, can't say she was that thrilled about it, but she had to agree. I also said we need to see inside Eleanor's room, and

68

she said she'd find out if that was possible, but I'm not holding my breath.'

'I'm nearly ready, Shirley,' Noah's breathless voice called back. 'I've just got to brush my teeth and then I'll be down.'

'You don't need to brush your sodding teeth every time you leave the bloody house.' Shirley rolled her eyes. 'Come on, we've been through this before. No one is going to be in a rush to smell your breath, are they?'

Teeth-brushing sounds ensued, and her brow furrowed. For God's sake, she suspected her new assistant had obsessive compulsive disorder. His little habits were becoming more obvious now that she was actually trying to get things done.

'I'm going to start the car,' she said loudly. 'If you're not out in five, I'm going without you.'

Shirley was feeling like a new woman this afternoon. The last remnants of the hangover had subsided and so had the anxiety – for now at least. A sort of euphoria had taken her over instead, a glowing anticipation at the prospect of delving into this case. It was the biggest she'd taken on yet, and she wasn't thinking about just the payment. Which, let's face it, promised to be enormous. Her sparsely numbered previous clients had mainly wanted her to investigate more mundane things, like background checks for errant employees, breach of privacy laws and fraud. She'd had one man wanting her to find out about his wife's affair – it turned out she wasn't even having one, which had been an anti-climax. But a death with suspected foul play – at least suspected by the victim's father? Now that was taking her to a whole new level. If she could just work through this successfully, she knew in her bones her private detective agency would get off the ground at last, when word of her reputation spread...

Six minutes later, Shirley and Noah were cruising down her narrow Winslow road, with Shirley squeezing her dented midnight-blue Vauxhall Corsa expertly between double-parked cars. The houses on either side were modest constructions, mostly red-brick and semi-detached. She cranked the volume of the radio up, but Noah put his hands over his ears, so she rolled her eyes and turned it down to a semi-loud volume. Soon, they were speeding down the A413 towards Buckingham, with Alice Cooper screaming as their soundtrack.

'Can you slow down a bit, please?' Noah said, staring straight ahead.

'Nope,' Shirley said. 'Your bloody teeth-brushing held us up, and I want to get to the university before the students and tutors start fucking off home.'

Ten minutes later, the Vauxhall Corsa was turning right off the Brackley Road, and on to the grand, straight – exceedingly long – drive that led up to Royal Buckingham University.

'Bloody hell, it's a bit posh round here.' Shirley indulged in a few glances left and right, quickly taking in the rolling green grounds that were heavily punctuated by stone arches, decorative ruins, pretty ponds and a bunch of other pointless but pleasing stuff. 'Lucky students, having all this on their doorstep, eh?'

'It's nice. I like it,' Noah said, gazing out of the window.

'You would,' Shirley said. 'I always knew you were too classy for your mum's council estate. Posh sod.'

They arrived at an understated sign pointing them left into a car park. Minutes later, Shirley had heaved herself out of the driving seat, and the pair walked up a gravel lane towards the imposing, sprawling main university building.

'Looks like it was built in a mixture of styles.' Noah screwed his eyes up as he peered at the gigantic structure. 'Which probably means it was added to over the centuries. If I had to guess, I'd say it was a mixture of English baroque and Palladian, judging from that Ionic tetrastyle portico.'

Shirley stopped puffing up the path for a minute and turned to stare at her nephew.

'How the hell,' she said, 'do you know this stuff, Noah? If I had to describe this mansion I would say it's big and fancy with lots of arches and columns. But you come out with a frigging architectural history complete with poncey terminology. Honestly, how do you do it?'

Noah paused, and shrugged.

'I just never forget information,' he said. 'If I read something, or listen to details in a documentary, I simply store them away in my brain in case I need to access them again later on.'

Shirley raised her eyebrows.

'Blimey,' she said. 'That's a real gift you have, you know? You might be more useful to me than I realised. My memory's like a broken bloody sieve.'

Acknowledging Noah's small, proud smile, she turned back to the path.

'Come on then,' she said. 'But walk slower this time, will you? It's not easy being five feet four and over twenty-four stone. Makes hiking a bit difficult, if you know what I mean.'

As they neared the vast wooden door, only one of several entrances along the building's extended façade, it burst open and a balding man sporting a bright green velvet jacket appeared.

'Can I help you?' His voice was loud and his accent was plummier than the Queen's.

Shirley stopped, wheezing slightly, planting both her feet wide apart on the path.

'Yeah,' she said. 'We are here to investigate the death of Eleanor Parkhurst, the student who so unfortunately died here yesterday.'

A range of emotions flitted across the man's face, ending in a frown.

'Are you with the police?' he asked, the disdain in his voice suggesting that he very much doubted it. 'They have ruled Eleanor's tragic death an accident. And I have not been informed of any further investigations by other parties.'

Shirley wiped her sweating hand on her coat, then proffered it forward.

'Let's start from the beginning again,' she said, not taking her eyes away from his for a second. 'I'm Shirley Butterworth from Justice Investigations. I'm a licenced private investigator, and this is my assistant, Noah.' The man reached forward and shook her hand for the merest second. *He has a limp grip*, Shirley thought. *Papery and weak.*

Noah made a guttural sound in his throat by way of greeting.

'Eleanor's father,' Shirley went on, 'has employed us to investigate her death further. He's not satisfied by the autopsy report.' She fumbled in her pocket and retrieved a battered ID card showing her credentials. 'Part of my duties here involve interviewing witnesses and conducting research into what went on. Can I ask your name please, sir?'

'Van Bern,' the man said. The way his expression was closing down greatly interested Shirley. 'Professor Eric Van Bern. I'm the head of the arts faculty. Eleanor was one of our students.'

'Well, isn't it lucky I bumped into you then, Professor Van Bern?' Shirley said. 'I do believe it would be hugely helpful to talk to you, if I may? Do you have time for a quick chat now?'

'Oh, er–' Van Bern shifted up his jacket sleeve to stare at his watch. 'Actually, I'm just off to...'

'I'm sure you understand how hard all this is for Mr Parkhurst.' Shirley's voice was loud and firm. 'If we could all just work together to bring him peace of mind he would be forever grateful, I'm sure. I won't take up too much of your time, sir, but the quicker we get on with this, the earlier I can get out of your hair, as it were.' She looked at the sparse remnants of hair on the man's head and immediately regretted using that particular idiom. She cleared her throat, and gave what she hoped was a bright, professional smile.

Eric Van Bern sighed, and gave her a look addled with contempt.

'Fine,' he said. 'I can give you ten minutes, but no more. Agreed?'

'Perfect, thank you,' Shirley said. 'That will be a great start, Professor.'

He turned back towards the door and motioned for them to follow him.

'We better go to my study,' he said.

Shirley ushered Noah in front of her, and took a few seconds to look about her before following him. All she saw were trees, a ruined arch, a line of bushes, a pond, grass, carefully tended flower beds, and two pigeons strutting across the path. Which was disquieting. Because the whole time she'd been talking to the odd man, Van Bern, Shirley had had the strangest feeling that they were being watched.

18

———

S *hit*, Dillon thought, from his spot behind the row of large evergreen shrubs. He'd been for a deliciously long run that morning – all the way to Padbury and back – and was now busy weeding. He'd been digging down deep into the earth, attempting to excavate the roots of a particularly stubborn yarrow, when he'd spotted the enormous lady with the bright red hair and her nerdy sidekick walking up towards the house. With secrecy being second nature to him, he'd automatically concealed his presence in order to watch them. People interested him, they always had. He liked to understand everything he could about them, and to get to the bottom of what made them tick. Invariably, much of that information would benefit him at a later date.

What he'd just overheard had shocked him, rattled him in a way most things didn't nowadays. Of course, he'd heard on the grapevine that Eleanor's autopsy report had come back saying she'd died by accidental drowning. Everyone at the university knew, it was all anyone was talking about; not much remained a secret round there for long. He'd been relieved when he'd heard that, especially after what happened when Eleanor had stayed behind with him after the Satanic meeting on Wednesday night... But now Eleanor's father wanted her death investigated further?

Dillon knew that what had happened on Wednesday wasn't his fault, he hadn't done anything wrong, but that bolshie private detective he'd just seen probably wouldn't see it like that. He knew she wouldn't let things lie if he told her what had gone on between him and Eleanor. He shook his head, an unexpected stream of anxiety making him lose his clarity of thought for a minute. No, he wasn't having that. His mind was everything to him. He needed to find peace quickly, there was no way all of this was going to mess with his brain.

Turning away from the evergreens and weeds, Dillon picked up his shovel and started off over the grass in the direction of his small cottage, his lanky long legs walking rhythmically. Skunk always gave him peace of mind and helped him order his thoughts. It was why he smoked so much of it. The feeling was amazing, the way his mind cleared into a deep understanding of everything. He visualised rolling himself a big fat spliff as soon as he got in. Yes, he nodded to himself. That would sort him right out. And he might allow himself to go for another long run later.

Also, he thought, nearing his house, there was now the immediate need to hide certain things away from prying eyes. If the detective came round, poking her nose in to his business and asking questions, he was going to make sure there was absolutely nothing of interest lying around for her to see... Satanism – he knew – could send even the most rational human being into a Satanic panic as soon as they encountered it. Just hearing the word made people freak out and reach for their rosary beads. Most of the public, the sheep of the world, just didn't understand Satanism, and that was the problem. Their social conditioning just wouldn't let them scratch the surface of it, and allow them to look more thoroughly into what was actually the most sensible belief system ever created; the only one that truly made sense. And Dillon's own work of art, New Satanism, was the best version of all Satanic groups in existence. Because at its heart, it embraced evil as well as good – a fact he was only just beginning to filter down to his followers. And this detail was so necessary, yet overlooked by all the other more mainstream Satanic temples and churches. But Dillon knew that without embracing the dark as well as the light, people constantly felt guilty about everything. They were always trying to be 'nice' and do the right thing. Whereas in reality, humans weren't just good, they were bad and evil too; a whole kaleidoscope of every emotion and intention. Denying all of that was to deny important parts of yourself, to repress your true being. What most people never realised was that it was okay to be bad sometimes. It was human nature. It was Satanic nature. And what he'd been up to recently, in the privacy of his own home, certainly showed this... *Yes, he thought. If that redhead appears with her little helper, all she's going to find is a small cottage, with absolutely nothing exciting – or incriminating – inside it...*

19

S eth stared at his cell wall opposite him. He'd been here for two hours now, ever since the pigs had picked him up in Maids Moreton. He'd walked blindly up to that village after leaving his mum's – all the way up steep Moreton Road; he'd had no plans in his mind at all at that point, just knew he needed to get away from everyone. And, *of course*, his mum had pressed criminal damage charges against him, stupid, treacherous bitch, when she'd found the house in the state he'd left it. Couldn't put herself in his shoes for once, could she? Think that maybe he was really traumatised because his beloved girlfriend had just died. That woman had no loyalty to anyone or anything, he knew, except to her addiction of drugs and alcohol. In hindsight he probably shouldn't have smashed up the living room on his way out of the house, but his anger had been too strong, too all-consuming. Eleanor was dead and there was nothing he could do to change that.

The thought made his fists curl and he brought them down hard either side of him on the thin mattress that smelled pungently of disinfectant. Hot tears splashed down his cheeks. He could feel his thoughts splintering in his head, it was a physical sensation, it hurt as much as it would if his leg or another part of his body broke apart. How had things come to this? He hit his closed eyes hard with the heels of his hands. A week ago, life had been so good. So full of promise. So full of Eleanor.

If she was no longer alive, then he didn't want to be either, Seth realised, opening his eyes. Now that he'd been arrested, and rejected by his mum, and betrayed by his Satanic leader, Dillon, there was nothing left for him. Mainly, he knew he was ashamed of his actions on Wednesday night. If he hadn't done what he had, Eleanor would probably still be alive. He didn't deserve to live anymore. He was filled with such shame, such guilt and remorse, that the skin all over his body felt hot, like it was burnt. He needed to join Eleanor right now, in whatever Heaven or Hell she was in, make sure she was okay. He looked around, then down at his body. His shirt was ripped, he hadn't even realised until now. Must have happened when he was destroying his room. Taking it off, he worked away at it, pulling and ripping, feeling the burning of the effort on his hands, until much of the fabric had been divided into rough strips. He tied the strips together, creating one long ragged rope, and looked around. Now, where could he tie it to? Somewhere that would hold his weight?

The problem with police cells, he thought, a stab of annoyance running through him, was that they were designed to stop inmates from doing precisely this. But he was going through with it one way or another, now that he'd committed to the idea. A sense of urgency flooded his mind; he wanted to get on with it before anyone came to stop him. No half measures, he wanted out.

He looked up above his head. There was an air vent. It was small, but he might be able to do something with it. Standing up on the hard bed, Seth pushed the metal grille as firmly as he dared. He didn't want to make any noise, the last thing he needed was a copper poking their head in. The grille wobbled a bit, but held fast. Seth took a deep breath, then pressed harder. With a metallic noise, one corner of the thin structure gave way, and he was able to gently prise the rest off. He chucked the grille on the bed, and reached up to feel around in the small hole in the ceiling. His fingers touched something cylindrical, and he gripped it firmly, pulling it a bit to test it for strength. A pipe, and a sturdy one at that.

His mind now clear and calm, Seth carefully fed one end of the ragged fabric through the hole. His fingers prised and pushed until he could feel it feeding around the pipe. He grabbed the end and pulled hard; it was secure. Tying the ends together, he fashioned a noose, making sure it was high enough to hold him off the ground. It was important that he didn't muck this up, like he had with the rest of his life. If he could do one thing right, he thought, it would be to successfully die without a hitch.

Satisfied that he'd done the best job he could, Seth put the noose around his neck and shuffled to the edge of the bed. He breathed in and out, enjoying the last bodily sensation he would ever have. Hearing a door open further down the corridor, Seth said a silent goodbye to his stinking life, and jumped off.

20

———

Shirley was wedged uncomfortably into a ridiculously small ottoman chair in Eric Van Bern's study. Noah was sitting beside her on a swivelly office chair, his breathing shallow and excited. She was watching Van Bern flapping around the room, pointlessly rearranging things on his shelves, pulling out bits of paper and then putting them back somewhere else. She'd already got him to fill in the personal details form, but the man had set off around the room after that. Watching his movements was making her dizzy. She cleared her throat.

'Would it be all right, Mr Van Bern,' Shirley said, 'if you came and sat down at your desk? It's just that I'm an old-fashioned kind of gal and I find I can concentrate better in an interview if the person is sitting opposite me.'

'An interview?' Van Bern hissed the words out. 'So that's what this is now, is it? You initially said we were having a chat, I believe.'

'Informal, of course,' Shirley said, as he reluctantly lowered himself into his study chair, without making any eye contact with her. 'Like I said, we are just here to find out what really happened to Eleanor. Perhaps it was an accident, perhaps not.

80

As you know, Mr Parkhurst would like us to take a more thorough look, for his own peace of mind, and I'm going to need your help in order to be able to do that. Now, perhaps you could start by telling me what Eleanor was doing on Wednesday, in the hours leading up to her death. We will talk to as many other people as possible too, her friends, classmates, tutors and that, but it would help if you gave us as much information as possible to start with.'

Van Bern folded his fingers together and stared at the ceiling.

'As far as I understand it,' he said, 'Eleanor emailed a below par essay to her tutor Daniel in the early hours of Wednesday morning, before sleeping off her efforts. I have no idea what she did when she awoke, but it has become apparent that in the evening she attended a society with her friends in the school grounds. Her friends apparently lost track of her after that, and then at some point, as we know, she tried to make her way back to her hall room. It was a freezing night, and very dark. She slipped over, hit her head and drowned in the pond.' Van Bern shook his head slightly, and Shirley was taken aback to see tears shining in the corners of his eyes. 'Such a tragedy,' he said softly.

'Thank you,' Shirley said. 'Were you particularly well acquainted with Eleanor, Mr Van Bern? I can see how upset you are getting, and I'm sorry to have to go through this with you.'

'No, we didn't know each other well,' Van Bern said, glancing out of the window. 'But Eleanor was such a lovely girl, filled with great promise – as, of course, all our students are. It's simply shocking that her life was cut short like this, that's all.'

'Yes.' Shirley nodded slowly, staring at him. 'Absolutely. Now, you mentioned that Eleanor attended a club on Wednesday night. What was that about then?'

Van Bern tapped his fingers on his desk for a moment, then turned to his computer.

'I believe it was one of our more wacky societies,' he said, clicking various buttons. 'But before I go into it, I'm just going to bring up Eleanor's student profile to give you absolutely accurate information and times. All her essays and marks, as well as her extra-curricular activities, are recorded on there.'

'Jolly good.' Shirley nodded. She turned to Noah, and whacked him on the knee. 'Come on, look lively, slowcoach,' she said. 'Where's that notebook you brought with you? You need to be earning your keep, boy. You should be making notes by now.'

She turned back to Van Bern and saw his eyebrows raise slightly.

'Ah yes, here we are,' he said, as a page of information flashed into being on his screen. 'A log of Eleanor's activities. So on Wednesdays' – he ran his finger down the list – 'it appears that she was attending the New Satanism Society in the ruined temple, from eight to ten in the evening.'

'Come again?' Shirley said, leaning forwards. 'The new what?'

'The New *Satanism* Society,' Van Bern repeated, as though explaining something to a two-year-old. 'Like I said, one of our quirkier clubs, but as a university we believe in celebrating diversity, and if we allow other religious groups to run, it was only fair that this one had a place too.'

'Yes, but...' Shirley said, trying to find the right words, images of blood and child sacrifice running through her mind. 'Satanism? I mean, isn't that kind of wrong?'

'How so?' Van Bern said loftily, leaning back in his chair. 'The founder of the society has explained to us that he uses Satan merely as a symbol of rebelliousness over arbitrary authority.'

What the fuck does arbitrary mean? Shirley thought, nodding. This guy was on another level if he was about to justify having a Satanic society at the university, she thought. What the actual hell? – no pun intended.

'Those of us that are on the pastoral committee questioned the founder of the society, Dillon Rushwell, quite extensively about his intentions, when he first brought his proposal to us,' Van Bern went on. 'Dillon was very well prepared, he presented us with a variety of literature about modern Satanism to read, and although I personally reject organised religions myself, I did find some of the Satanic beliefs quite compelling.'

Shirley stared at him, her mouth staying slightly open despite her best efforts at closing it. She could hear Noah scribbling away beside her.

'You mean you *liked* some of the Satanic beliefs?' she managed at last.

'Well, that is a rather ignorant and simplistic way of interpreting what I've just said.' Van Bern closed his fingers together. 'I didn't say I actually *liked* their beliefs, I said I found them compelling. Interesting, worth contemplating. Because in essence, they are common sense – they centre around individual self-worth, rejecting pointless authority, and questioning everything. And as an academic' – he allowed himself a small smile here – 'I have to say that these are tenets I've been adhering to my whole life.'

Tossing academics, Shirley thought, aware she'd started grinding her teeth while he was talking. *So up themselves it's unreal. Absolutely full of shit. Ignorant and simplistic my arse.*

'Thank you for explaining that, Professor Van Bern.' She forced a smile, making a resolute decision to do some research of Satanism herself when she got home. It was just a word – Satanism – but it was loaded with so many cultural and religious evils – literally – she thought. Against her better judgement, as every detective knows it's of paramount importance not to jump to conclusions in cases, Shirley found herself already making associations with Eleanor's death and this Devil-worshipping society, even though she had to admit she knew next to nothing about it. *Stop it, Shirl,* she said to herself. *This Satanic thing is just one starting place for the investigation, that's all. You need to keep an open mind.* 'So you say Dillon Rushwell runs the club?' she said. 'He is obviously someone I'll need to speak to. Do you have the names of Eleanor's friends that she went with, as well?'

'No, I do not,' Van Bern said, standing up. 'But I can inform you that her tutor was Professor Daniel Weatherby, and if you speak with him he will be able to provide you with a list of her fellow classmates. Now, I believe our ten minutes are well and truly up. So if you'll excuse me, I have more important things to do.' He walked over and opened the door, then stood next to it like a sentry.

Shirley nodded and heaved herself out of the chair. She didn't like Van Bern at all. He came across as all flamboyant and clever, but there was a general air of insincerity about him. It was as though he didn't know who he really was, so he had to project an air of careful contrived-ness to the world instead. A slippery eel if ever she'd met one. *But you mustn't let your personal feelings affect you, Shirl,* she cautioned herself. *Objectivity is the key word here. Okay, so he's a bit of a twat. Keep a cool head about you, all right?*

'Thank you for your time,' she said. 'I'll know where to contact you if I need to speak to you again. Come on, Noah, bring the notebook and let's get going. Just one more thing,' she said, pausing and turning to Van Bern. 'Could you tell me exactly where Eleanor's body was found on Thursday morning? I've read all the information Mr Parkhurst has sent me about this, but it would be super amazing if you could pinpoint the exact spot for us while we're here.'

'Yes, a member of my department, Doctor Abigail Dahiru was the unfortunate, ah, discoveree of Eleanor's body,' Van Bern said. 'She was on her way to our faculty meeting, and spotted the girl faced downwards in a pond that lies near the staff car park to the back of the building. You'll find it easily, many of the students have left flowers and cards there out of respect for the poor girl. It's turned into quite a shrine.'

'Fantastic, thank you,' Shirley said, squeezing past him, with Noah at her heels. 'We'll find it. I'm sure we'll meet again, Professor Van Bern. But until then, goodbye.'

'Hopefully we won't, Miss Butterworth,' he said softly, closing the door as the pair of them started off down the corridor.

'What a wanker,' Shirley said under her breath a few seconds later. 'Did you notice, Noah? He barely looked me in the eye once? He's a slippery fish, you mark my words.'

Noah nodded.

'I didn't like him very much,' he said.

'You and me both,' Shirley said with a grimace. 'Right, let's make our way out of this bloody maze of a building. We now need to locate the exact spot where Eleanor died.'

21

Dillon blew a smoke ring, then another. The skunk was working its magic, and he was already feeling better – his thoughts were gaining clarity by the second. As always, his friend – the Devil – was helping him, guiding his beliefs and feelings, telling him what to do next. It was as though he had a pipeline to Satan in his brain, he was so lucky to receive these messages from the prince of darkness. It was why his society, New Satanism, was the best of all Satanic movements. Everything about it came from the source, the one and only, the big man himself; Lucifer, Beelzebub, whatever you wanted to call him. Dillon grinned, all anxiety now gone. He looked down at his naked chest, enjoying his favourite tattoo – the Devil horns, emblazoned above his nipples. Sometimes it felt like him and Satan were one and the same being, as though the antichrist had taken over his body – or more accurately – melded his self with Dillon's soul. He laughed, a vision of how wonderful things would be when he'd fully disclosed all of this to his followers. When they were ready. Which would be soon, but not quite yet...

He looked over at his Satanic shrine – his careful assemblage of a skull, candles, books, pentagrams and statuettes. He knew the demonic mystery it emanated was the same as the power he himself wielded. Strong, dark, shadowy and commanding. And oh-so addictive. Making Devil horns with the hand that wasn't holding the spliff, he prayed to Satan for deliverance from the snooping eyes of that red-headed private detective woman, and from anyone else who came sniffing around. The Devil would understand, Dillon knew he would, as He'd already made it clear that He had much greater and grander plans for him. There was no way He'd let him get in any trouble now.

Dillon felt the power of the Devil enter him with force. He shut his eyes, enjoying the climactic sensation; honestly, he thought, power is almost better than sex. Although maybe it's the same thing, at the end of the day, an all-consuming conquering and ejaculation of supremacy. He needed the energy Satan was pumping into him in order to clear up a few loose ends tying him to Eleanor. He took a deep drag, held it in his lungs for several seconds, then exhaled. He stubbed out the end of the spliff in the nearby ashtray and stood up.

Walking over to the leather sofa, he bent down and pulled out a storage box from underneath it. It was pretty much empty, which was good, as in a few minutes it would contain all his notes that he'd made about Eleanor, since spotting her at the university the first time. Her routine, what she wore, where her room was, what he'd learned about her family – she was adopted, her mother had died in a crash, her father was now in a wheelchair and was overprotective. They were his notes, his property, for no one else's eyes. They'd been part of his vision for his future plans for Eleanor, and now they wouldn't be happening, of course. It was a shame she'd died, but he felt no grief. He embraced the dark in life, it turned him on, in fact. Maybe Eleanor was with Satan now, looking after him, helping to guide him, protecting him. Yes, he thought. She probably was.

With all the notes now in the box, and several files and notebooks – taken from the nearby shelf – piled on top of them, Dillon placed the wicker lid back on it and slid it back under the sofa, pushing it as far as it would go. Later this evening, he thought, he would do some research of his own. Look up the rights of private detectives on his laptop, see what authority they had on searching people's houses. He wasn't worried, he knew the police believed Eleanor's death was accidental. It just seemed to be the big woman who was poking around, and he was pretty sure she wouldn't be able to get a warrant to search his home. But even so, it was always better to be prepared.

Right, he thought, picking up his neatly folded black vest and pulling it on. *Time to go and see my 'other' clients in Buckingham. The ones no one at the university has the faintest clue about...*

22

Hunter walked slowly towards the reception desk at the hospital. He glanced upwards and caught sight of the clock: it was nearly half past seven. Thursday had turned out to be a very long and painful day indeed. He'd found out about Seth half an hour ago, and moved heaven and earth to get straight to the hospital, managing to convince a guy from down the corridor to give him a lift into Milton Keynes. Seth needed someone there, he couldn't go through all this alone. And he felt ashamed to admit to this, but he also had an ulterior motive for visiting; he wanted to find out how much Seth knew about what had happened on Wednesday night... what he, Hunter, had done...

But hospitals, like police stations, gave Hunter the creeps. They were so institutional, so bland, everyone was wearing uniforms and moving purposefully around. He knew he stood out like a turd in a punchbowl, standing there in his leather jacket, his long hair down his back, his eyebrow ring shining in the artificial light, while busy doctors, nurses, visitors and patients moved efficiently around him. He felt awkward, a lump of difference in a sea of sameness. But he was prepared to feel uncomfortable for a moment or two if it meant he could find his way to his friend.

A few minutes later, the tired girl at reception had located Seth's ward and given Hunter directions to it. He set off through the maze of bright corridors that all looked the same, wondering what state Seth would be in when he found him. Spotting a sign for Ward K, he stopped and peered through the window in the nearest door. Yes, the sign on the wall inside told him this was definitely the right place. He pressed the buzzer, and a distracted nurse let him in, before turning and walking off again.

Walking into the room, Hunter saw six beds – three on either side. Most of them were occupied by middle-aged or elderly men, all white-faced and ill-looking. One of them was coughing relentlessly, while another stared into the middle distance, unmoving. Then there was Seth, in a corner bed. He was lying down, his eyes closed. Hunter blinked, for a moment wondering if his friend was actually alive – he looked so still and lifeless. He walked over to him.

'Hi, Seth,' he said quietly. There was a mask over his friend's nose, attached by a tube to a big tank labelled 'oxygen'. A ligature mark – an angry red line, about an inch and a half thick – ran around the middle of his neck. It was grazed and lacerated in places and looking at it made sick rise in Hunter's throat. How bad must Seth have been feeling to do this to himself? he wondered.

'Seth?' he said again. He watched his friend's eyes flicker and open. A range of emotions and realisations flitted across them in quick succession: hazy, to shocked, to panicked, to confused. Was this the first time he'd regained consciousness? No, surely not, Hunter thought. But his thoughts were still obviously disordered about what had happened, about what he'd done. Waking up must be a shock every time.

'Hey, it's okay, mate.' Hunter took Seth's hand and held it gently. 'I've just come to visit you. How are you doing?'

Seth's hand went up to his face and he pulled the oxygen mask down to his chin.

'I'm alive,' he said. 'Although I'm not sure I'm glad about that.' *His eyes look haunted*, Hunter thought. What must it be like to try and kill yourself, only to find out you've failed?

'You certainly gave us all a scare there.' Hunter gave his friend a small smile. 'If it makes any difference, buddy, I'm glad you're still here. Don't go doing something like that again, do you hear me?'

Seth stared at him, then turned his face away, wincing as he moved his neck.

The same nurse that had let Hunter into the ward bustled over.

'Ah good, I'm glad you've come to see him,' she said with a smile. 'He needs some really good friends right now. If he'd been hanging there for a few minutes longer, he wouldn't be with us anymore.' She turned to speak to Seth. 'And I'm sure your friend is as glad as all of us that you're still with us.' Her voice was kind as she spoke. Seth didn't meet her gaze. The nurse turned back to Hunter. 'A policeman found him in the nick of time. When they cut him down he was unconscious, apparently. He's had a brain scan and spinal X-ray, and there doesn't look like there will be any lasting damage, so we are expecting him to make a full physical recovery. Maybe you can help support him with the mental one?'

Hunter nodded, and the nurse smiled and walked away to talk to another patient.

'Look, mate,' he said to Seth. 'I'm so sorry you were feeling bad enough to do this to yourself. Eleanor dying so suddenly like that must have hit you hard. It shocked all of us to the core, we all feel broken. I just want you to know that I'm here for you, buddy. You don't have to go through this on your own, okay?'

Tears started cascading from Seth's eyes. He said something but the words were too mumbled for Hunter to hear.

'Sorry, can you say that again, I didn't quite catch it?' Hunter leaned closer to his friend.

'I said' – Seth's voice was cracked and husky – 'that it's my fault Eleanor is dead. That's why I don't deserve to live anymore.'

Hunter stared at him.

'What do you mean it's your fault, mate?' he said.

Seth's crying was in full flow now.

'When I left the student bar that night, I was so angry with her,' he said in gulps. 'I thought she must still be with Dillon, because she never came to meet us like she said she was going to. I loved her, Hunter, I really did. And I was planning on telling her that on Wednesday after the meeting. But she chose to stay with Dillon rather than coming to see me. She ruined everything – we would have been so happy together. I felt so fucking mad, I knew I needed to have it out with her, so I headed back towards the ruined temple. When I found her, she was walking away from the temple, up the path towards the main building. I just ran up and gave her both barrels, I told her she was a bitch and a slut who didn't care about anyone but herself. I said she was just a selfish little rich girl who had everything she wanted, and she didn't know what life was really about; that she didn't know how to love or be loyal. I was really horrible to her, Hunter, but I was so hurt I couldn't stop, I just kept talking. Then she started crying, and I told her to go fuck herself, and ran off home.'

'Okay,' Hunter said slowly. 'I understand you were in pain that evening, and the drink probably made you say more than you normally would have. But why do you think you killed her?

You just told me she was crying when you left her, which means she must still have been alive?'

'Yes,' Seth said, wiping his tears. 'But don't you see? I must have made her so upset that she got in a real state and wasn't concentrating on where she was going. If I hadn't had a go at her, she would have got back to her room safely. But because I made her so sad she must have lost her way and fallen. *That's* why it's my fault she's dead.'

Hunter was quiet for a moment, thinking, his insides relaxing. So Seth knew nothing about what else had happened that night. He would have mentioned something, if he was aware of anything out of the ordinary. But what his friend had just told him certainly helped to explain a few things; like why Seth had felt so bad he tried to top himself. And why Eleanor was crying when he – Hunter – had seen her that night, after he'd left the bar following yet another argument with Natalie. But he wasn't going to tell Seth, or anyone else for that matter, that he'd met up with Eleanor late on Wednesday night. No one needed to know that. Not after what had happened last time with that girl. There was no way he was ever going to let himself be locked up again. He needed his freedom like he needed air to breathe. But he also had a conscience, and he didn't want to see his mate suffering like this. He'd started to think of Seth as the little brother he'd never had; felt strangely protective of him.

'Listen, Seth,' he said slowly, his voice low. 'You need to get the idea that you're responsible for Eleanor dying properly out of your mind. It wasn't your fault, buddy, I can promise you that. And I'll tell you why. Word at the university is that a private detective showed up this afternoon. Hired by Eleanor's dad, apparently, who doesn't believe his daughter's death was an accident, like the police think it was. Her dad seems to think she was murdered, and the detective must agree or she wouldn't have turned up. So that bit of information gets you right off the hook. Because like you say, she was alive when you left her, therefore it wasn't anything to do with you that she died. So stop beating yourself up about it.'

Seth's eyes were wide, staring at him.

'Eleanor was murdered?' he said, his voice a rasp.

'That's what Eleanor's dad thinks anyway,' Hunter said with a nod and a sigh. 'So stop blaming yourself. Eleanor wasn't perfect, and she shouldn't have done what she did on Wednesday, staying behind with Dillon like that. But I know for a fact she wouldn't want to see you like this. She *did* care about you, Seth, even if she had a funny way of showing it. So get yourself out of this state, mate. Look forwards, not backwards. Stay strong.'

'Poor Eleanor.' Fresh tears sprang from Seth's eyes, but the muscles in his face had relaxed a bit.

'Yes,' Hunter said. He looked down. 'She didn't deserve what happened to her. But you've been given a second chance, mate.' He looked up again. 'So don't blow it. Get yourself better, and start living a life that makes Eleanor proud of you. She's watching, remember, from her new place in Heaven.' *Or maybe Hell...*

23

‘I don't know about you, Noah, but I'm knackered,’ Shirley said, relaxing back into her favourite old armchair. ‘Oh, be a love and chuck me a bar of chocolate from the cupboard, will you? I'm starvin' marvin'. That burger meal we got on the way home barely took the edge off. And I think I'm ready for a small glass of wine again.’ She shot him her best, most winning smile.

‘I'll get you the chocolate, but not the wine,’ Noah said seriously. ‘And I'm not telling you where I've hidden all the bottles, so don't ask. You're much nicer when you're not drunk or hungover, you know, Shirley. And in any case, we've got a big job on at the moment and we can't allow your alcoholism to mess it up.’

‘Oh for God's sake, Noah, how many times do I have to tell you, I'm not a bleeding alcoholic,’ Shirley said loudly. But a voice in the back of her mind questioned how truthful she was currently being. ‘Fine,’ she said with a sigh. ‘Just get me the bloody chocolate then. At least I can comfort eat if you won't let me get pissed.’

Half an hour later, she had demolished three quarters of a family-sized bar of milk chocolate and was working on disposing of the rest. Noah had decided to read out the notes he'd taken during their day's work at the university.

'At the site of Eleanor's death,' he read, 'there are many flowers, cards and gifts obscuring the ground where she lay. We studied the visible area as best we could, and also investigated that stretch of the pond, where she was found face down. The depth of the water measured twelve inches at its deepest, and two at its most shallow. I told Shirley we should take the temperature of the pond, but she said, "I can tell you the temperature right now, it's fucking freezing degrees", but I measured it anyway as I had brought my thermometer with me...'

'Yes, all right, Einstein, you don't need to record every single little thing I say,' Shirley said, grinning as she chewed. 'Just the important bits.'

'And the temperature turned out to be four degrees,' Noah went on. 'Two degrees higher than the air temperature, which I happen to know is caused by thermal circulation within interacting ground water...'

'Just the relevant facts, please, clever clogs, I don't need a science lesson.' Shirley rolled her eyes as she popped the last piece of chocolate into her mouth.

'We conducted a careful search of the grass and water,' Noah continued to read. 'And aside from the expected natural elements, the only unusual object we found – at the bottom of the pond – was a very small silver buckle. I asked Shirley if she thought it was an important clue, and she said "Maybe, who knows, bag it up anyway, will ya?" So I did. We were not able to see the rock Eleanor allegedly hit her head on as the police had taken it away.'

'Very good, Noah,' Shirley said, catching him looking at her expectantly. 'Especially the direct transcript of my speech. By the way, where's the buckle now?'

'I created an "evidence" folder, using the stationery you told me to buy earlier,' Noah said. 'I couldn't find a Dictaphone by the way, it seems there's not much demand for them in Winslow, but that's all right because I bought several notebooks instead. I put the bag containing the buckle in a plastic folder; it's in the file now, all labelled and dated. If you let me tidy your desk this evening, I can...'

'No, not today,' Shirley said, thinking of the important bit of hidden information she needed to check on. Why the hell hadn't she found the time to do that yet? 'I need to go through a few things before you do that. Just give me a day or two. Anyway, you deserve some downtime now, Noah. You did well on your first proper day as my assistant.' And the good thing was, she reflected, they'd been so busy today she'd hardly thought about Tiffany at all. A stab of pain immediately ricocheted through her, and she shook her head. No, she wasn't going to give in to the hurt now, just because she'd thought of her name...

Noah smiled, his cheeks flushing pink.

Shirley's phone, resting on the arm of her chair, sprang into life with a series of beeps, its *Star Wars* ringtone soon filling the room.

'It's Mr Parkhurst, Eleanor's dad,' she said, looking at the name that was flashing up. 'Go and make yourself useful somewhere else, while I have a chat with him, will you, Noah? I find it easier to concentrate when you're not staring intently at me.'

A few minutes later, she switched off her phone, putting it back on the arm of the chair, staring at it for a few seconds.

'Noah?' she shouted in the direction of the stairs. 'Better get yourself off to bed soon, we've got an early start tomorrow morning. Mr Parkhurst wants to meet us in person at his house, says he's got a few things to show us that might help our investigation. Looks like we'll be leaving for Sussex at the crack of dawn. And then in the afternoon we need to go back to the university and find as many people as possible who knew Eleanor. Tomorrow's going to be a busy day, my boy.' *And today's not over for me yet,* she thought, pulling her laptop on to her knee. *It's time to properly study that autopsy report and research the delightful Satanism movement...*

24

———

Dillon had been enjoying himself in Buckingham town for hours. He'd only come down to give his regulars their skunk – and collect their payments, too, of course – but one thing had led to another, which surprised him, as he usually controlled his day carefully, and he was now sitting in the graveyard by St Peter and St Paul's church, with a gang of people he barely knew, a can of lager in his hand. Satan was obviously giving him permission to relax for a bit, let his hair down, as it were. But he better keep an eye on himself, it wouldn't be good to get out of the rhythm of his carefully planned life. The sky had been dark for a while, which meant it must be getting very late. He should be getting back soon, he'd planned to find out more about the rights of private detectives, hadn't he? Forewarned was forearmed, and all that...

He looked around at the assembled mass slouched in a semicircle about him, their faces glowing softly in the beams cast by the lights on the church's spire. Dillon knew he was intelligent. He didn't have the academic kind of cleverness like those ponces at the university did, his unique brainpower had been honed on the street; he had the ultimate kind of intellect –

99

he understood people, and how they worked, and he understood life. That kind of knowledge was way better than anything books could teach you. And he knew his learning had given him an almost supernatural ability to compartmentalise, the way he'd been around the block, lived in different places, adapted to multiple circumstances. He was a different person to so many different groups of people, and none of them had any idea about the 'other' Dillons, the faces and personalities he showed elsewhere. To the university staff, he was the groundsman who was good at fixing anything and everything, a quirky character who ran a little club in the ruined temple. To his Satanic followers he was their leader, someone to look up to, to try and be like. To his clients in Buckingham town – mostly teenagers and hard-faced young twenty-somethings – he was their dealer, a Jack the Lad, who liked the easy banter he shared with them. To his parents... well. It didn't matter because he hadn't seen them, or his sisters, since his mum had chucked him out all those years ago. And to Satan, he was the chosen prince of darkness, who was ready and willing to follow out the plans shown to him. He was a chameleon, a maverick. No one knew the real him. He had more secrets than anyone would ever know. And he loved it that way.

'Do you want some of this, Dillon?' a girl sitting near him was saying, holding out a joint. She was gazing at him with a mixture of awe and admiration; Dillon was used to it, it was how most females looked when speaking to him. She was quite pretty, in a girl-next-door kind of way, but she wasn't his type. He winked at her anyway though. Never pass up some free attention, he thought. He couldn't help his magnetic aura, could he? It was always there, exuding off him, and that's just the way it was.

'Well, I was just about to get going' – he flashed his most mischievous smile – 'but since you're offering...'

'Hey, didn't someone die at the university yesterday?' A guy sitting to his right with lip and eyebrow piercings asked, turning towards him. 'My aunt works in the canteen there, and she told my dad something had happened.'

Dillon exhaled a thick line of smoke.

'Yeah, apparently someone was found dead in the grounds,' he said lazily. 'A girl called Eleanor. I'd seen her around, but I didn't know her or anything. Never spoke to her...'

25

———

It was half past nine on Friday morning when Shirley's Vauxhall Corsa pulled into the drive of Alistair Parkhurst's Sussex home, High View House.

'Blimey,' Shirley said, staring through the windscreen, rubbing her eyes. She regretted staying up so late now, studying all the information Mr Parkhurst had emailed her, together with Noah's notes about what they'd learned during the day. She'd taken a good look at the autopsy report, and was leaning towards Eleanor's dad being right about the involvement of foul play. The head injuries and haemorrhage didn't seem consistent with an accidental fall to her, there was something about the multiple placements of them that just didn't seem to be consistent with a simple trip over, but she'd emailed a physician who specialised in traumatic brain injury, asking if he could help her out, and also what his fee would be. Hopefully not too much, she hardly had any spare cash...

The research that had eaten into her sleeping hours the most had been her investigation into Satanism. When she'd started, she'd been totally revolted by the notion. She hadn't been brought up in a religious household, and typically didn't have any truck with any of that nonsense. It freaked her out, if she was honest. It wasn't right, large organisations telling you what to think and how to behave. It took away from free will, brainwashed people and made them unable to think for themselves about what was really right and wrong. She'd found that in the UK the main Satanism movement was called The Temple of Satan; she'd spent ages watching YouTube videos of their rituals, as well as interviews with members, and part of a really odd documentary. By half past one in the morning she was feeling quite frankly bloody confused about Satanism. Because according to all the people involved with The Temple of Satan, who incidentally and bafflingly all seemed rather nice – the type she'd like to go out for a drink or three with – they didn't worship the Devil at all. They used him as a symbol against authority. They never sacrificed children or anything else, and they didn't think it was okay to harm anyone. In fact, many members had set up helpful community groups, like litter-picking ones, or after-school clubs. So why the fuck did they have to wear Devil horns on their heads when they did all this nice, benevolent stuff? Why make themselves look weird to everyone else in the world? Mind you, she'd always felt different from the masses, so who was she to judge them? She wasn't immune to the stares she received due to her size, but she'd learned to laugh them off, or ignore them. In the end, she'd found the contact details of the chapter head of the UK's Satanic Temple, a guy going by the name of Lucifer Johnson, and pinged off a message asking if he would meet her for an interview. Then she'd slammed the laptop lid down and gone to bed.

'Nice view, eh, Noah?' she said, looking around, wishing she'd bought herself three coffees at the petrol station instead of one. And a can of Coke and anything else with caffeine in it.

Rolling Chichester countryside fell away from them on either side, consisting of carefully manicured fields in shades of brown and green. Beautiful trees were dotted throughout the view, their branches bare now that winter was approaching. Beyond the grasslands lay the sea, glittering peacefully in the cool November sunshine. She'd visited Sussex a few times before, had friends in Brighton. Had spent many happy days with them on the pebbled beach there, enjoying crispy food cooked on disposable barbeques in the sun. But Chichester was another world. It was gorgeous, so serene. And by the looks of the other houses they'd passed, you had to have a ton of money to afford to live anywhere near it.

'Right' – she shook her head, attempting to bat away her exhaustion – 'let's get on with it then, Noah, shall we? Don't want to keep our client waiting.'

Seconds later they were trudging over the gravelled drive towards the imposing arched front door, which opened before they reached it. A dour-faced man sat in a wheelchair in the doorway, staring at them with hooded eyes. An air of hopeless defeat radiated from him, which wasn't surprising, Shirley reflected, seeing as he'd just lost his only child. The man looked from her to Noah, then offered out his hand, unsmiling.

'Alistair Parkhurst,' he said. 'You must be the detectives. Do come in.' His gaze, for the briefest of seconds, took in Shirley's car, but his expression didn't change.

After the initial greetings had finished, Shirley and Noah followed the man through the spacious hall and into a fair-sized study. Mr Parkhurst positioned himself behind the desk and motioned for the other two to sit in the leather chairs in front of it. Shirley glanced around, taking in the plethora of photos that featured a pretty, smiling blonde girl in almost all of them. Eleanor. Eleanor riding a horse, Eleanor wearing a snorkel, standing in the middle of a bright blue sea, Eleanor laughing with another girl, Eleanor cuddling a rabbit, Eleanor standing in front of the Eiffel Tower, young Eleanor in a school uniform.

The girl had certainly led a privileged life, that was for sure. But none of that was of much use to her now, was it? Bless her poor heart.

'As you can imagine,' Mr Parkhurst said, 'my daughter's death has caused me unimaginable amounts of pain. And it always will.' His voice reminded Shirley of a bit of withered wood; it was dry and cracked, as though every word he spoke could be his last. 'There is nothing left for me on this earth now, I shall merely wait out my days. But I have made her a promise, and that is to investigate the circumstances in which she died fully and precisely, so that the truth comes to light, and she may rest in peace. Do you understand?'

Shirley nodded.

'Of course,' she said. 'I do, Mr Parkhurst. And let me just say that we are both so sorry for your tragic loss.'

Mr Parkhurst nodded his acceptance of her sentiments. 'If you would ever have had the good fortune to meet Eleanor, you would understand more fully why her loss is so particularly devastating for me. She was more than merely a beautiful girl, she was perfect in every possible way. Composed, engaged, intelligent, kind, caring, and, of course, she had model looks. She wasn't my biological daughter, you know. My wife and I adopted her when we found out we couldn't have children of our own.' His face lit up for a fraction of a second, and Shirley digested the brief glimpse she saw of the man he used to be.

'Oh really?' Shirley said, glancing at Noah. She was glad to see he'd opened his notebook and was starting to write. Good, the boy was learning.

'Yes.' Mr Parkhurst nodded. 'It was a closed adoption through the council, we never learnt the identity of her biological parents. Which didn't matter a jot, because once we brought Eleanor home when she was just three weeks old, she felt like ours. Although I do think,' he said, his jaded eyes dimming, 'that I seemed to take more naturally to parenthood than my dear, late wife.'

'Oh?' Shirley said, hoping he'd carry on with this thread. The more she could learn about Eleanor's background the better. All information was vital and important.

'Well, Emmeline – my wife – was a very social person, and was never happier than when she was out entertaining others at a dinner party or soirée,' Mr Parkhust said. He stopped, and let out a big sigh. 'The problem was, that she didn't want to curb her lifestyle when Eleanor came to us. I often wondered whether she would have reacted differently if she'd actually given birth to the child, you know, gone through the pregnancy process herself, etcetera. Perhaps she would have bonded more with the baby then. But as it was, well. After a month or two, she began making it clear that little Eleanor would have to fit round her needs, rather than the other way around. So I stepped in, and became the main caregiver in many respects. Of course, I'd fallen head over heels in love with Eleanor as soon as I saw her, so this wasn't a chore for me, it was a natural instinct. I just always felt Eleanor would have benefitted from having a closer maternal connection, you know?'

'Mmm,' Shirley said, nodding, willing him to go on. She heard the scratch of Noah's pen, pleased he was continuing to take notes.

A look of bitterness shadowed Mr Parkhurst's face for just a second.

'Of course, Emmeline was having numerous affairs,' he said, seeming to force his expression into neutral once more. 'There was never anything I could do to stop her. When she was older, Eleanor started to copy her mother's coquettish behaviour with men. It drove me mad the way she learned how to flirt, to wrap them round her little finger, just like Emmeline did. It was too painful, I tried to stop it, had very hard words with Eleanor indeed. She was *mine*, not Emmeline's, and I didn't like seeing anything less than perfection in her, because it didn't need to happen. Do you understand? It was unnecessary. She was just copying her mother, but in reality she was so much better than that.'

'I see,' Shirley said, her voice a murmur. She was beginning to get a much clearer picture of Eleanor and her family already. Mr Parkhurst seemed to be talking about his daughter as though she was his possession, rather than an enabled separate individual. But one thing was certain, he'd certainly loved the girl to bits, and was clearly devastated by her death.

'You mentioned before, Mr Parkhurst,' Shirley went on, 'that your wife passed away at some point. That must have been hard on you and Eleanor in many ways?'

'Yes it was.' Mr Parkhurst's expression turned hard. 'Although the accident was Emmeline's doing. It was her fault. If only she'd listened to me, and been reasonable, that horrendous event could have been avoided entirely.'

'What do you mean?' Shirley said. 'What happened?'

'Emmeline and I were driving back home, after having spent an evening with friends, Aubrey and Milo,' Mr Parkhurst said. 'Eleanor was sixteen at the time, a wonderful girl, really excelling at school. She had a group of really lovely friends at that time, all from good homes, of course. I'd known for some time that Emmeline and Milo were having an affair; I was so used to Emmeline's behaviour that that fact in itself didn't bother me too much, as long as she was discreet about it. I had Eleanor, and she was all I needed. But during the dinner party, Emmeline drank far too much and became very vulgar and reckless, continuously making inappropriate remarks about what she and Milo had been up to. His wife, Aubrey, didn't care at all, of course. She thought it was funny, as she herself slept around when she felt like it. They had an open relationship of sorts. Fuelled by too much gin, in my opinion. But for me, my wife's behaviour that night was too much; it was one humiliation too many. I demanded that Emmeline leave with me, after she'd spewed out a particularly insensitive comment, so we got into the car and set off on the twenty-minute journey home.'

Shirley nodded, waiting.

'Of course, I was angry,' Mr Parkhurst said, through gritted teeth. 'I had every right to be. Emmeline had embarrassed me too much, her behaviour that evening was inexcusable. And in addition to that, I was sick of her lack of care of Eleanor, tired of the way Eleanor had begun to copy her mother's flirtatious ways. This stress had been building in me for some time, as you can imagine, and Emmeline's behaviour at our friend's house had been the last straw. I shouted at her as I drove, told her exactly what I thought of her. And then she lashed out at me, hit me across my face. But she did it at a moment when I was trying to follow the curve of the road round a tight country bend in the dark, I was going faster than I should have, but I was incensed with the woman. As her arm came across my face, it obscured my vision, and I drove off the side of the road. The car, with us in it, tumbled down a sheer cliff face, only stopping when it crashed into a tree. Unfortunately Emmeline's side of the car took the greatest impact, and she was killed immediately. And as you can tell,' he said, with a grimace, 'I lost the use of my legs in the accident. And life has never been the same since.'

'I'm so sorry, Mr Parkhurst,' Shirley said, meaning it. She'd been through enough troubles in her own life, but this man had really had it hard. 'It must have been awful for Eleanor, to learn about what happened to both of you.' All the same, she thought. He was coming across as though he was completely unable to take any responsibility for his part in the terrible crash, however unacceptable his wife's behaviour had been.

'Yes.' Mr Parkhurst blinked, but tears leaked from his eyes

anyhow. 'It devastated her. She and Emmeline were never particularly close, but she did love her mother, and was inconsolable at the loss. And with me becoming disabled overnight, when Eleanor had been cosily tucked up in bed, expecting to see her parents at home when she woke up the next morning, well. It was as though she took on the role of being my primary carer immediately. She stopped her silly ways with boys – which pleased me immensely – and stayed at home instead, doing everything she could to help me. She was an angel. Which is why it was so hard for me when she decided to go away to university.' His gaze dropped.

Shirley stared at him, many thoughts tumbling through her mind. *Yes, it must have been hard on you,* she reflected. *But have you any idea how tough things must have been for your daughter? You seem to have wanted to be the centre of her world, without allowing her to grow up and live her own life. You are coming across as a tad self-centred, Mr Parkhurst.*

'Am I right in thinking Eleanor was studying for a master's at the Royal Buckingham University?' Shirley said.

Mr Parkhurst nodded.

'Yes, she was,' he said.

'Where did she get her bachelor's degree, the same place?' Shirley said.

'No.' Mr Parkhurst shook his head. 'Luckily, I managed to convince her to study from home for that one. She went to the University of Chichester, just around the corner. Still lived with me, and looked after me in the evenings. She gained a very respectable 2:1 in History of Art, and I was extremely proud. It was just so hard when she said she'd been accepted on a master's course at Royal Buckingham University...'

'Yes,' Shirley said. 'I'm sure it was. Now I have to ask you, Mr Parkhurst, did you ever meet any of Eleanor's friends from Buckingham? In order to find out what exactly happened to her that night, I'm going to need to speak to as many of them as possible.'

'I never met any of them, but she told me all about them,' he said. 'We had daily chats on the phone – long ones – and she told me about Seth, Natalie and Hunter, and what a nice group they all made together.'

'Seth, Natalie and Hunter,' Shirley repeated. *Good*, she thought. *Now we're getting somewhere.* She could hear Noah scribbling away beside her. 'Did Eleanor also tell you about the society she'd joined at the university?'

'Eleanor didn't have time for clubs or societies,' Mr Parkhurst said. 'She was a dedicated student, always getting top marks. She told me herself she wouldn't let anything get in the way of her studies.'

'Ah,' Shirley said. 'Well, she did join a club, Mr Parkhurst, we have the information from the head of her faculty, it's recorded on her student profile.'

'Oh?' Mr Parkhurst's brow furrowed. 'What was it? An art-related one, I'll bet.'

'Well, actually, it was rather an unusual one,' Shirley said. 'You know what students are like, always experimenting with different ideas. The society she joined was called New Satanism.'

'Satanism?' Mr Parkhurst said, his pallid face turning a shade whiter. 'You are telling me my daughter joined a club that worshipped the Devil?'

'I don't know.' Shirley sat forward. 'I don't know what they do at the society, but please be rest assured that I'm going to find out.'

'This is preposterous.' Mr Parkhurst glared at her, then banged his fist on his desk. 'My daughter wasn't a Devil worshipper, Miss Butterworth. And I think I know her rather better than you do. I'll thank you not to come into my house with such ridiculous and malignant notions in the future.'

Shirley stared at him, considering her next move. She needed this job so badly...

'Of course,' she said. 'I'll go and check the facts again, make sure that what her head of faculty told me is correct. There may well have been a mistake. Don't you worry, Mr Parkhurst, I'm the best there is. Your case is safe with me, I'm going to do everything in my power to find out exactly what happened to Eleanor. Now while I'm here, if you don't mind, can we discuss the first down payment, please, I'm going to need it for resources...'

26

Seth lay on his back, staring at the ceiling of Hunter's room. After being discharged from the hospital – following a psychiatric evaluation, and a date for a follow-up appointment – his friend had taken him in, told him he could stay there as long as he wanted. After finding out about her son's attempted suicide, his mum had dropped all charges against him. But he didn't want to go back to hers, it was too toxic in that house. He just felt angry all the time when he was there. No, he wanted to move on from that. He needed a fresh start, and he had to be away from her for that to happen. Hunter was right, he had to look forward, not back now; make something of his life.

Seth had been feeling an increasing lightness enter his heart and body over the last few hours; it was almost a euphoric feeling of clarity, one he'd never had before. And he hadn't even smoked any weed or drunk any alcohol – he'd decided to knock all that on the head for the time being, until he'd got himself straightened out. No, the euphoric feeling was to do with surviving near death, and the future possibilities he could see for himself now. He had a chance to lead a good life, to become positive and strong, and make something of himself. Maybe in the future, he could find a way to help other people, like the doctors and nurses in the hospital had helped him, and like Hunter had. And he had his mate to thank for his realisation of that; Hunter was wise, the things he came out with. He was out at a class now, with Natalie, although the two of them seemed to be barely on speaking terms these days. Seth was having a break from his studies, Hunter had helped him sort it out with the university powers that be. He needed a bit of time to regroup and heal. And think.

He had to admit, he was still a bit annoyed with Eleanor – for staying behind with Dillon on Wednesday night – but mostly he felt sorry for her. Whatever had happened to her that evening was awful, she hadn't deserved it. No, the person he hated now was their stupid Satanic leader, Dillon. If Eleanor had been murdered, it made sense that Dillon had something to do with it. After all, he was always going on about how marvellous the dark in life was, how it was important they were free to explore the bad in life as well as the good. Seth had gone along with all that at the time, because he was desperate to fit in with the group. But he felt different now, it was weird. Almost as though his suicide attempt had made him grow up a bit, made him feel more himself. There was no way in hell he was ever going to follow Dillon again. He was never going to another one of those stupid meetings, he'd never wear black eye make-up and make Devil horns with his fingers, no way. And he found he was constantly questioning everything Dillon had already told and taught him. Instead of just accepting it, he was wondering if any of it held any value. Or had Dillon just been talking out of his arse the whole time? Making it up as he went along, with his only intention being to reel his followers in so he could dominate and control them? Maybe none of it was true, maybe it was all a load of crap. When he'd seen Dillon invite Eleanor to stay behind with him that night, Seth's opinion of the leader had started to change. Dillon had disrespected him, he hadn't cared that Eleanor was his – Seth's – girlfriend, he'd been quite happy to overrule him on that, throw it back in his face. But then, why had he been surprised? Seth wondered. Dillon always said he was bad as well as good. So why would he care about hurting someone like that? He probably got a kick out of it, got off on it.

So what he *did* want to do – Seth rolled over, the pain in his neck making him flinch – was to find out if Dillon had had anything to do with Eleanor's death. She'd looked upset after she'd left the ruined temple, not that he'd cared at the time. What if Dillon had followed her afterwards and done something to her, when he'd walked away? Seth didn't know exactly how or what he was going to do yet, but that was okay, he had all day to think. There must be some way to find out what had happened to Eleanor on Wednesday night...

27

'Well, here we are again,' Shirley said, pulling into Royal Buckingham University's visitor car park. She drained away the last bit of her extra-strong large coffee – a vital and much needed purchase from their most recent petrol station stop. Their meeting with Alistair Parkhurst that morning had been a strange experience, and she'd come away with a lot to mull over. As well as a hefty deposit in her account, a down payment for necessary resources, which was brilliant as she'd now be able to pay the head-trauma expert, if he got back to her with the go-ahead. And several new photographs of Eleanor, and other bits and bobs to do with her schooling, hobbies and former childhood friends. And she'd been surprised to find – when returning to her car in Mr Parkhurst's drive – that Lucifer Johnson, chapter head of the UK's Satanic Temple, had already emailed her back with a rather sweet message, suggesting they meet up in London the following Tuesday. So she'd pinged him a note back agreeing. The more she could learn about Satanism the better. Then she'd phoned ahead to the university, and got the head honcho's secretary, who'd said no there was no news on whether Shirley could inspect Eleanor's room, which was now locked and off-limits to everyone except the police. She'd have to get in there sooner or later, Shirley thought, there would no doubt be important evidence in there that had been overlooked, especially since the coroner had so hastily ruled Eleanor's death an accident...

'Come on, Noah, let's go and find out who runs the New Satanism Society,' she said. 'I have a feeling that the events of Eleanor's last night may start to become clearer when we speak to whoever that is.'

Ten minutes later, after questioning several students and members of staff about who ran the Satanic society, they had been pointed in the direction of a small stone cottage on the edge of the grounds. Apparently they needed to speak to Dillon Rushwell, the groundsman and general odd-job guy, who ran the society from some building in the grounds called the ruined temple. Reaching the cottage, Shirley approached the thin wooden front door and rapped sharply three times. Good, the subsequent noises from within meant that this Dillon character was home. She glanced at her watch, it was quarter past three. Crikey. They'd already accomplished a lot, and the day was far from over yet. But bloody hell, she needed more caffeine; tiredness was beginning to make her feel pissed off.

A beautiful-faced man opened the door and smiled. His long brown hair was wound up in a topknot and his bare arms were covered in ink. A sweet smell of incense wafted out either side of him.

'Hi,' he said in a husky voice. 'Can I help you?'

Shirley paused for a minute, wrong-footed. For some reason, she'd been expecting an older, rough-looking man, not this tattoo-covered gorgeous piece of flesh. She'd personally always been attracted to girls, but was willing to admire a perfect male specimen when she saw one.

'Ah, yes,' she said. 'We're looking for Dillon Rushwell?'

'You've found him,' the man said, his eyes sweeping from hers to Noah's. 'How can I help you?'

'I'm Private Detective Shirley Butterworth, and this is my assistant Noah,' Shirley said. 'We're investigating the death of Eleanor Parkhurst, and we've been told she attended a society you run on the evening that she died. Would it be all right to come in for a quick chat?'

'No problem.' Dillon held the door wide open for them. 'Come in. Ask me anything you want, although I'm not sure I'm going to be much help.'

Minutes later they were all sitting in Dillon's sparse and tidy little living room, Shirley and Noah squashed together on the little two-seater sofa, Dillon gracefully perched on a wooden stool.

'Right,' Shirley began. 'Talk me through this society, if you would, Mr Rushwell. I'm an old-fashioned kind of gal, and not very well acquainted with the world of Satanism. If you could explain what it's about, what draws people to it, who attends, and most especially what Eleanor did during your session on Wednesday night – I would be much obliged.'

'Wow, that's a lot of points to address.' Dillon's eyes crinkled playfully. 'I'll do my best. Let's see, so what is Satanism about? Well, I guess the best way to explain it is that it's a new religion, for people who want to think outside the box. It's not about child sacrifice, like most outsiders seem to think...'

'That's a relief,' Shirley said. So far so good, his definition fitted in with what she'd read the night before.

'We use the Devil to symbolise rebellion against pointless authority,' Dillon went on. 'For us, the Devil is someone who questions the status quo, which is exactly what we do.'

Shirley whacked Noah, who was staring intently at a pile of objects on a small table near Dillon.

'Come on, slowcoach, get that notebook out,' she said. 'Christ alive, I would have thought you'd have learnt by now.'

Dillon followed Noah's gaze.

'Ah, he's looking at my Satanic shrine,' he said with a smile. 'Don't worry, there's nothing evil about it, it's just made up from some symbolic and ritualistic objects I like to look at when I'm meditating.'

Shirley stared at the skull. *Personally, I'd rather look at a bottle of wine*, she thought. *But each to their own.*

Noah fumbled in his pocket and pulled out the now dog-eared notebook.

'That's better,' Shirley said, as her nephew began scribbling. 'Go on, Dillon.'

Dillon told her about the tenets they went by in New Satanism, about how individual and free thought was so important, and for a wild moment Shirley found herself warming to the sound of the society. *It's strange*, she mused, *but what he's saying all makes sense, like everything I read last night did, at least on the surface. But don't be fooled by external appearances, Shirl. Look deeper. What is it that this man is not telling you?*

'Do you have a list of everyone who attends your club?' she said, when Dillon had finished explaining. 'And any information about it?'

'Yes I do,' Dillon said. 'It will take me a minute or two to get, if you are all right to wait?'

'Absolutely,' Shirley said, watching him unfold his legs and stand up. 'And if it's not too much bother, could you make us a coffee while you're there? I'll take mine white with three sugars, please.'

'Shirley,' Noah said, turning to her. 'You can't just demand...'

'It's fine,' Dillon said with a grin. 'No trouble at all.'

They watched him walk out of the room. Noah frowned at

Shirley, who nudged him back, causing the pen to fall from Noah's hand. It rolled under the sofa.

'Bit dusty under here,' Noah said, as he got onto his hands and knees to retrieve it. 'The room is tidy enough but Dillon's obviously no good at thorough cleaning. Although there's a storage box under here that's obviously been moved recently, it's made a clean pathway through all the dust.'

'Has it indeed?' Shirley said, leaning forward. She glanced at the door, then back at Noah. 'Quick, pull it out then, and let's have a look while he's not here. We need more information, and Dillon here is coming across a bit too good to be true.'

Noah's expression was one of horror.

'But we can't just go around sneaking into other people's stuff without their permission,' he said.

'Listen, my boy, that's exactly what we need to do,' Shirley hissed, her face very close to his. 'We are looking into a possible murder, and are in the house of a Satanist. Now get that frigging box out quickly before I whack you one.'

Noah reached under the sofa and slid the box to where she could reach it. Shirley quickly took the lid off and rifled through the contents.

'So many papers and books,' she muttered. 'Ah,' she said. 'What do we have here?' The name 'Eleanor' – written on a pile of paper at the bottom of the box – caught her eye. She quickly grabbed the stack of papers, stuffing them into her bag, throwing in one of Dillon's notebooks from the box, too, for good luck. Then she popped the lid back on, and Noah, furtively looking over his shoulder at the door, quickly slid the box back into its original position.

'Good thing I've got you with me,' Shirley said in a low voice, elbowing him in the ribs. 'Not many people would notice the pattern of dust under a sofa like you, eh, Noah? The fact that you're a cleaning machine comes in useful in more ways than one. I'll have to get you to dust under all of my furniture when we get home, eh?'

Noah grunted, then bent his head over the notebook, obviously wanting to look busy when Dillon came back, and Shirley picked up a book that was lying on the coffee table.

'*The Satanic Bible*,' she read out loud, as Dillon came back in carrying a tray that held three steaming mugs. He had a large notebook tucked under his arm. 'Looks like a barrel of laughs. Is this your bedtime reading then, Dillon?'

Dillon smiled as he handed her the coffee.

'It's a classic in the world of Satanism, actually,' he said, sitting down again. 'Written by Anton LaVey, who founded the Church of Satan many years ago. My society – New Satanism – is different from his in many ways, although there are some similarities.'

'Oh yes, how so?' Shirley said.

Dillon explained about the fact that you have to pay to belong to the Church of Satan, whereas his group was, of course, free to those who wished to join, and how they met regularly whereas the church did not. Shirley watched him as he talked, trying to work out what to make of him. She felt like his papers emblazoned with the name 'Eleanor' were making a hole in her bag. Oh, how she wanted to see what was written on them, to see if anything incriminating was on them, but she'd have to wait and be patient. He obviously wasn't telling her the whole truth, as he hadn't referred to them, so there must be something written on them that Dillon wanted to keep hidden. There was a large possibility that the man in front of her was a master manipulator, she decided. Coming across as sweetness and light, saying all the right things, and being charming. While all the time he'd kept secret notes about Eleanor in a box under his sofa. If they were perfectly innocent notes, why wouldn't he have shown them to her? Jesus, why were people so complicated and dishonest sometimes? At least Noah was straightforward, she thought. His comments were so honest that some of them felt like a punch in the face, but at least you knew where you were with him.

'So talk me through Eleanor's last night with you,' Shirley said when Dillon had finished talking. 'You're a very important witness, you know, Dillon. For all I know you may be one of the last people to ever speak to her, so do go into as much detail as you can, will you?'

'Of course, not a problem,' Dillon said. 'So Eleanor and her friends turned up at the ruined temple as usual on Wednesday, at around eight in the evening. We had a great session, using all the props I'd brought with me, then I closed it down around ten. She stayed behind to help me tidy everything away, and she asked me more about the annihilation ritual I'd suggested we try the following week. She was only there for about twenty minutes, then she went on her way. She said she was going to meet up with her boyfriend at the student bar. That was the last I saw of her.'

'Her boyfriend?' Shirley's ears pricked up. Mr Parkhurst hadn't mentioned anything about that. But mind you, there seemed to be quite a lot he didn't know about his daughter. 'Who's that then?'

'Seth,' Dillon said. 'Seth Hamilton. Might be worth trying the hospital in Milton Keynes if you want to speak to him. I heard he got arrested and tried to top himself yesterday.'

'Arrested?' Shirley said, her tone sharp. Mr Parkhurst had mentioned the name Seth, she remembered, but just as one of Eleanor's 'nice' friends. 'What for?'

'No idea,' Dillon said. 'Just what I heard on the grapevine. You know how news gets around in a place like this.'

'Well, thank you, Mr Rushwell,' Shirley said, standing up and putting her empty mug back on the tray. 'You've been extremely helpful. I'll contact you again if I need more information.'

'Please do,' Dillon said, standing up to show them out.

Dillon stared at the odd pair as they tramped back towards the university in the darkening gloom. That had gone much better than he'd been expecting, he mused. He was pretty sure he'd won the old girl over with his frequent smiles and habitual allure. No one could resist him, he was unstoppable. So desirable. He suspected this was due to the way his good looks contrasted with the Satanic energy he exuded. People love a bit of conflict, he thought, a bit of dark and light. Heaven and Hell, good and bad. Pain and pleasure. Most people couldn't get enough of it. It was because they denied the dark in themselves, so had to live vicariously through him. And Satan had answered his prayers and looked after him as usual; he was pretty sure that detective and her weird sidekick wouldn't be back again – he'd given her a list of attendees of New Satanism to go away with, along with a stash of photocopies about Satanism that showed it in its most palatable light. *Joke's on you, Shirley Butterworth*, he thought with a grin, as he closed his front door. *You'll never know the real Dillon Rushwell, or what went on the night that Eleanor died. But have fun trying to find out...*

28

Natalie sat alone in the student bar, nursing her third pint of lager. Her insides felt like they were torn to shreds, she didn't know what to do. Hunter was carving a memorial to Eleanor, and he said it was going to be his best work yet. It had almost killed her to see the care and love he was ploughing into it. Why did he have to do that? Why couldn't he just concentrate on her – Natalie – instead of putting all his energy into stupid Seth and dead Eleanor? She took a big swig and realised she hadn't eaten anything that day. No wonder she was feeling so light-headed all of a sudden. But food didn't interest her at the moment.

A movement to her left caught her attention, and as she turned she saw a giant redhead of a woman pass by the window, followed by a tall, scrawny teenager with black hair curtains. *Weird*, she thought. *I've never seen them around here before. Maybe that's the detective people are talking about. Doesn't look much like one though. She looks more like a chef from the canteen.*

She couldn't take Hunter's indifference to her anymore, Natalie realised, draining the glass, and getting up to order another one. She just couldn't hack it anymore, couldn't take the emptiness it caused inside her. She was going to break up with him. Today. What had happened with Eleanor had been like a bombshell, had fractured their group apart. Seth tried to kill himself, and Hunter was there for him, rather than for Natalie, who had told her boyfriend in no uncertain terms that she was also shaken to the core by Wednesday's events. But he wasn't supporting her; it was like there was an emotional force field keeping him away from her. So, although it would nearly destroy her to do it, she was going to tell him she wanted to break up with him. She needed some peace in her brain, rather than the eternal angst and fear of rejection that was currently permanently in her thoughts. It was better to reject him first, rather than wait for him to do it. She'd just have a bit more Dutch courage, then she'd go and find him.

29

Shirley stomped down corridor after corridor, Noah jogging behind her. Where the hell was everybody? It was only four o'clock, surely the whole university hadn't already retired for the weekend. Mind you, it *was* Friday afternoon...

A door opened and a tall man with a distracted expression stepped out, almost banging into her. He was carrying a huge pile of folders.

'Oh, so sorry,' he muttered, turning the other way.

'Excuse me,' Shirley said loudly, striding to catch up with him. 'I was wondering if you could help us. We're looking for a student called Seth Hamilton. Would you know where we could find him?'

'Seth?' the man said, stopping to turn. 'Who are you? Why do you want to speak to Seth?'

'I'm Shirley Butterworth, I'm a private investigator, and this is my assistant, Noah.' Shirley gestured towards her nephew, aware that her speech was coming out in breathless bursts after all the unnatural amount of activity she'd been doing. 'We are investigating the death of Eleanor Parkhurst.'

'Ah, I see,' the man said. 'Well, I might be able to help a bit with that. I'm Professor Daniel Weatherby. Eleanor was one of my students. Such an awful tragedy, her dying like that.'

'Yes it was,' Shirley said, nodding. 'Do you have a few minutes to spare, Professor Weatherby? We need to talk to as many people as possible in order to find out exactly what happened to Eleanor that night, I'm sure you understand.'

Daniel nodded, and ushered them into his study.

'I thought the police concluded it was an accident?' he said, as the three of them sat down. He quickly filled out the personal details form Shirley thrust in front of him, his handwriting tiny and neat. 'Although my head of faculty, Eric Van Bern, did say a private detective was somewhere about on the grounds.'

'I've been hired by Eleanor's father,' Shirley said. 'He thinks it wasn't an accident. My job is to look deeply into the events of Wednesday night, to find out exactly what went on. So you were Eleanor's tutor, were you?' She reached up and wiped a line of sweat from her forehead.

'Yes, she was a student in my modern art master's class,' Daniel said. 'Seemed to be a popular girl, quite bright. Always handed her work in on time, and all that.'

'Could you give me a list of all the other students in the same class?' Shirley said. 'We need to talk to them too.'

'Yes, of course,' Daniel said. 'I'll print one off for you now.'

Shirley watched as he tapped away at his keyboard. The printer behind him whirred into life. He reached over and retrieved a piece of paper, handing it to Shirley, who passed it to Noah.

'Here,' she said. 'Put that away. I'll look at it later.' She blinked, her eyes returning to Daniel. 'So Eleanor was a good student, was she? Her father certainly seemed to think so too.'

'Yes,' Daniel said, nodding. 'She was. Although she seemed a bit distracted of late, which wasn't like her. Started checking her phone during class, and that sort of thing. And the last essay she handed in was well below par. I was a bit worried about her actually. I called her on Wednesday evening to try and discuss what was going on, but she palmed me off with an excuse or two, said she'd rewrite the paper.'

'You called her on Wednesday evening?' Shirley said. 'That's a bit unusual, isn't it? Don't you usually keep your interactions with students to work hours?'

'No,' Daniel said, with a small smile. 'I'm known as something of an ogre around here, Miss Butterworth. Ask any of the students or staff in this department. I learnt very quickly after starting work at the university, that students don't keep to normal office hours; they rise late and stay up all night. So I call them whenever I can, even in the evenings. In any case, this university is quite progressive in its teaching manner – we staff are here on Saturdays, too, as lectures start later in the day but are spread over six days of the week rather than five. I'm very careful about who I let on to the course, it's a popular one and I interview far more potential candidates than I can say yes to. I only give a place to those who show huge potential, and once they are here I don't let them doss about, I expect good work from them, and if they slack I'm on them straight away. They don't like it, but they are always grateful on graduation day, when their families watch them receive master's degrees with distinctions and merits.'

'Ah, you're an old-fashioned slave driver,' Shirley said with a smile. 'Good for you. We need more of those in education these days, if you ask me. You might still be in college if you'd had one of those, eh, Noah?'

Noah didn't look up, but shook his head and continued to take notes.

'This boy doesn't say much.' Shirley inclined her head at Noah. 'But he's turning out to be quite a useful assistant.

Anyway, you were saying Eleanor's academic performance was slipping a bit?'

'Yes,' Daniel said. 'Although normally, like I say, she was one of the best students. I have a video on my computer of her giving a presentation, if you'd like to see it? Get a better idea of who she was?'

'Yes please.' Shirley shuffled her chair forward. 'Everything helps. The more information, the better.'

Seconds later, she and Noah were gazing at the screen, watching the beautiful, confident blonde girl talk about Picasso's use of line. She felt a pang of sadness, seeing Eleanor as she used to be. The fact that such a vibrant young thing was now no longer on the earth was heartbreaking.

'Blimey,' Shirley said, after a few moments. 'I see what you mean. She's good at giving a speech. Obviously very bright.'

'Yes,' Daniel said with a sigh, turning the video off. 'Such a waste of a young life. So do *you* think her death was an accident, Miss Butterworth? Or are you inclined to agree with her father?'

'It's too early to say,' Shirley said. 'We are still investigating all leads. I will say that I've seen some evidence that suggests foul play was involved. To be honest, Professor Weatherby, some people we've interviewed are more forthcoming than others. And I have to say, you've been a lot more helpful so far than that Professor Van Bern. Having a conversation with him was like wading through tar.'

Daniel suppressed a smile.

'Eric has many funny ways about him,' he said. 'Perhaps all of us academics do. But I have to admit, he has been acting strangely since hearing of Eleanor's death. I wondered if it had anything to do with giving his own child up for adoption all those years ago. I imagine that's something one never really gets over. And we all knew Eleanor was adopted, she was quite open about it. I think that perhaps her death set off fresh grief in Eric about giving his own child away.'

'Yes,' Shirley said, looking over to make sure Noah was getting all of this. 'I didn't know Professor Van Bern had given up his own child. He didn't mention that.'

'No, well, he's a very private person,' Daniel said. 'And it's not usually the sort of thing people go around saying, is it? I just thought it best to mention in case you think his behaviour at all peculiar.'

'Thank you,' Shirley said. 'I think we'll be needing to talk to Professor Van Bern again in the near future, Noah. In actual fact, we've just come from Dillon Rushwell's house. Do you know him at all, Professor?'

A cloud crossed Daniel's face.

'He's not a person I like to spend much time with,' he said. 'Not that I ever need to. But I disapprove of all that Satanic nonsense. It fills the students' heads with rubbish when they should be concentrating on their studies. It's a ridiculous club to run here at the university. I don't know why the pastoral team allowed it.'

'I think Eleanor's dad would agree with you,' Shirley said, nodding. 'So you don't like Dillon very much then?'

'I don't know him,' Daniel said. 'But when I do see him, there's just something about him I don't like. He doesn't seem like a very honest person. Trickiness just radiates off him. If there's anyone you should be investigating round here, it's him. Don't ask me why I think that, it's just intuition.'

'Thank you,' Shirley said. 'And Seth Hamilton, Eleanor's boyfriend? Do you know him, or where we can find him? I understand he attempted suicide yesterday. Perhaps he's still in the hospital?'

'I believe he is back on university grounds, if what my students tell me is true,' Daniel said. 'If I was you, I'd try the bar.

People like Seth usually spend most of their time there, instead of studying for their degrees.'

'Brilliant,' Shirley said, heaving herself up. 'Thank you, Professor Weatherby, you've been really helpful.'

'Do let me know if you need any more information,' Daniel said, standing up and walking to the door.

'Oh, I will, don't you worry,' Shirley said. 'Come on, Noah, add that list of names to our stash of information and let's go to the bar. Don't forget the professor's personal information form.' *I could do with a drink myself*, she thought. *Not that that's possible with this alcohol policeman at my elbow every minute of the day.*

'It's in the basement,' Daniel said. 'Just take the stairs down and keep going until you can smell unwashed students.'

'Urgh.' Shirley wrinkled her nose. 'Sounds amazing. Right, let's go and see if we can find out what's happened to Seth...'

30

As they exited the stairwell, and Noah pushed open the glass doors, a waft of stale lager hit Shirley smack in the face. *Beautiful*, she thought, breathing it in. *I wouldn't say no to a pint right now, or better still, a bloody huge glass of wine. But no chance of that, so better not wish for something I can't have...*

'Where shall we start?' Noah said, raising his voice over the pounding music. 'There's quite a lot of people here.'

'Hang on,' Shirley said, looking around. 'Let me just observe the room for a moment. And you're still underage. Try to look older, will you?'

It was a big space, filled with different-sized wooden tables and benches. Low lamps hung from the ceiling, and there was a dartboard, two pool tables and a table football set up, all being used. The bar ran down the length of one wall; it was brightly lit and staffed by two guys and a girl, who were all busily engaged with customers. Shirley looked from table to table, trying to assess who best to go and talk to. One or two of the students were looking over at her and Noah, then nudging their friends and smiling. She was aware that she and Noah must stand out, but Shirley had felt like a square cog that had never fitted any round holes all her life, and she no longer much cared what people thought of her. She was used to causing a stir wherever she went. Noah, on the other hand, seemed to be trying to shrink back into the stairwell.

'Oh no you don't,' Shirley said, turning to him. 'This is part of being a private detective, Noah, talking to people. I know you hate social situations, but just think of yourself as being at work. And remember, it's important never to give a fuck about what other people think of you. Especially if they're being judgemental. So come on, grow some balls and get back beside me.'

Noah took a small step forward, and Shirley turned her attention back to the room.

A couple in the corner caught her eye – a big, long-haired man and a tiny, blue-haired girl. They seemed to be exchanging heated words, by the look of their red faces and gestures, but the music was louder than everyone's conversations, so she had no chance of hearing what they were talking about. *Perfect*, she thought. *A bit of passion. Let's start there.*

Pulling Noah's arm until he started following her, she set off through the tables, until she reached the one with the arguing couple.

'Mind if we join you?' she said, pulling up a bench before they could answer. 'I'm Shirley Butterworth, I'm a private detective, and this is Noah, my assistant. Come on, sit down, Noah, stop standing there like an idiot.'

The man and the girl had stopped talking and were staring at her.

'I'm investigating the death of Eleanor Parkhurst,' Shirley said. 'I was wondering if you could help me? We're looking for someone named Seth Hamilton.'

'Seth had nothing to do with Eleanor's death,' the big man said, his face like stone.

'Okay,' Shirley said, celebrating on the inside. They seemed to have struck gold here. She was glad she'd gone with her instincts. 'What's your name, mate? Don't worry, we're not accusing anyone of being involved with Eleanor's death, we just need to get a clearer picture of what happened.'

'Seth's in Hunter's room,' the blue-haired girl said. She was slurring her words together a bit.

'Shut up, Natalie,' the big man said, his brow furrowing further.

'Ah, so you must be Hunter?' Shirley said, with a smile. 'And you Natalie? It's great to meet you. Eleanor's father mentioned your names when we spoke to him earlier. Dillon might have, as well.' She wasn't sure Dillon had, but a bluff was as good as a charm. 'What luck that we've just bumped into you.'

Hunter glared at her. He didn't seem to think it was lucky at all.

'You've spoken to Dillon?' Natalie said. 'He was the last person with Eleanor, as far as I know.'

'Oh really?' Shirley said. 'Get your notebook out, Noah. So were you two with Eleanor on Wednesday night? Did you both go to the New Satanism meeting?'

'Yes,' Natalie said. Hunter's mouth stayed firmly shut. 'We always go there. Eleanor was late; I think she said it was something to do with her tutor phoning to complain about her work. Then afterwards, Seth got really upset because Eleanor wanted to stay behind with Dillon rather than come to the bar with us. He got really angry, actually, and drank even more than he usually does.'

Shirley felt Hunter's leg reach out under the table and kick Natalie's. The girl shifted position, moving out of his reach.

'I see,' Shirley said. 'Is that right? And what did you do after the New Satanism meeting, Natalie?'

'I came here with Hunter and Seth,' Natalie said. 'We waited for Eleanor for ages, but she didn't turn up. She was obviously having too much of a good time with Dillon. We all had quite a lot to drink, started doing shots and everything. Then Seth got mad and said he was going to find her. Then me and Hunter had an argument, as usual, and he walked off too. So I just went up to bed.'

'Thank you,' Shirley said. 'And where did you go, Hunter, when you left the bar?'

Hunter stared at her, his face blank and unresponsive. There was a pause of a few seconds.

'I went for a walk to clear my head,' he said. His voice was thick and low. 'I always do that when I need space to think. Then I went back to my room.'

'Alone?' Shirley said.

'Yes, of course I was alone,' Hunter said. 'You've just heard Natalie say she went to her room. And Seth didn't find Eleanor, so he went back to his mum's house in Buckingham town.'

'Ah, so he doesn't live in halls?' Shirley said.

'No, but he practically lives in Hunter's room,' Natalie said. 'They always play on the PlayStation together, it's really boring. Like I said, he's there now. Hunter took him in after Seth left the hospital. He tried to kill himself yesterday, tried to hang himself because he was so upset about Eleanor dying.'

'Can we go and have a word with him?' Shirley asked, standing up as though it was already a done deal.

'I already told you, Seth had nothing to do with what happened to Eleanor,' Hunter said, his voice a growl. 'Leave him alone. He's not well at the moment. He doesn't need you, or anyone else, poking their noses in.'

'Yes, and I understand that,' Shirley said, making her voice loud so it was heard over the music. 'But I still need to talk to him. As I'm sure you understand, Hunter, this investigation is very important – especially to Eleanor's dad. They wouldn't have released Seth from the hospital if he was too poorly, so don't worry, I'm sure he'll be fine with me having a quick word.'

Hunter kicked the table leg hard, causing the glasses on top to rattle, then he stood up.

'Stupid bloody detective,' Shirley heard him mutter under his breath as he walked past her.

Interesting, she thought, motioning to Noah to follow her. *So Hunter, Natalie and Seth were all supposed to meet Eleanor in the bar after the meeting, but she never showed up. And it seems as though Dillon was the last person to see her. Something in my bones is telling me that no one in this group is being completely honest with me. I need to get to the bottom of all this – get them to talk somehow. Right. Let's go and see what this Seth has to say for himself.*

31

Dillon's mind was imploding, and he hated how he felt. He couldn't control the waves of anxiety flooding through every part of his brain, because he didn't have the answer to his problem, and there was no one he could ask for help. Dillon was the master of his own destiny, a maverick, a chameleon who needed no one, who could be any different person at any time, depending on how he felt. *He* controlled life, not the other way around. Which is why the feeling of utter powerlessness brought on by discovering his papers about Eleanor were gone was utterly flooring him. Everything felt like it was going out of control. The room was spinning around him, he wanted to vomit. Even skunk wasn't helping.

'Fuck,' he said out loud. 'Fuck, fuck, fuck.'

Had Satan deserted him? he wondered. The powerful master who'd been sending him special thoughts for so long? Surely not. But he couldn't hear his friend the Devil now, no matter how hard he tried to listen. Where the absolute fuck were those papers? He'd put them in the box under the sofa, hadn't he?

Since Wednesday night, Dillon had been becoming increasingly worried about his mind. First, he uncharacteristically and spontaneously stayed out till the early hours of the morning in Buckingham with his skunk clients. This had made him tired the next day, and he hadn't been sure he'd removed all evidence of his love affair with Satan before that ridiculous detective had arrived. Now, he was even questioning his own memory, wondering whether he had actually put the papers about Eleanor under the sofa in the first place.

Yes, he decided after a few minutes, he had, he was positive he had. Surely that detective couldn't have found them? Stolen them from him without him realising? He hadn't been out of the room that long, and she looked like too much of a freak to be of any threat. And her sidekick looked next to useless. But still, it was looking like the only possibility. Maybe she was better than she looked...

He sat down, then stood up again. He relit his spliff and took some deep drags, trying to calm his mind. Now, if that Shirley Butterworth had probably taken his papers, and fuck knows what else, he was going to be in deep shit. He hadn't been honest with her about what had happened between him and Eleanor on Wednesday, because frankly, it was none of her business, and he answered to no one, especially amateur detectives. Okay, so yes, when Eleanor had stayed behind after the meeting that night – as he'd hoped she would, having thought of several possible scenarios the day before and how he could keep her there – things had happened between them. He'd offered her a spliff, which she'd declined, so instead they'd drunk absinthe together. She'd been gagging for him, literally offered herself to him on a plate, which he'd known she would. But it was about the game, not the conquest, Dillon knew. So he'd allowed her to think they were going to have amazing, mind-blowing sex together, had teased her, and wound her up to breaking point, but then he'd stopped abruptly, and told her she needed to leave.

'What?' she'd said, not believing him. 'What do you mean? Aren't we about to...?'

'No, I'm tired,' he'd said, enjoying watching her face fall, as the rejection took hold. 'I need to get home.'

So she'd got dressed, got her bag and left, shooting him an enjoyably hurt look on the way out. He'd followed her, wanting to see where she went. It was like he was the cat and she was the mouse. That's when he'd seen that person near the pond in the grounds. And that person had seen him, just for a brief second before Dillon had retreated back into the shadows, before turning round to get his belongings from the temple and going home. Now, if Eleanor had been murdered, which Dillon still wasn't sure he believed – because she could quite well have fallen and hit her head, especially after the absinthe, then he knew that he himself hadn't done it. She'd been very much alive as she'd walked away. And he hadn't seen anything happen to her. So while he didn't actually see this other person do anything, he'd bet money that they had something to do with it, if in fact Eleanor's death was a murder.

Which is why, he thought, *I'm going to pay that person a little visit now.* Dillon was no killer, but he knew that the ways in which he preyed on people, made notes about them, followed them, controlled and manipulated them, wouldn't go down well with the police. Not to mention his skunk dealing, and other little side businesses to do with coke and ecstasy. He wouldn't exactly come across as squeaky clean if a proper investigation was conducted. If that detective woman did have the notes he'd made about Eleanor, then the police would come after him, if she managed to prove Eleanor's death was a murder and not accidental. He *knew* they would. And there was no way he was going down for a crime he didn't do. No way in hell.

Ah, there was Satan again, guiding his thoughts. He knew He hadn't abandoned him. *Yes, thank you, Satan, I will go and have a little chat with that person,* he thought. *I need to find out their involvement with Eleanor that night. And if necessary, take appropriate action...*

32

'Fuck, what a day.' Shirley kicked her shoes off as she walked through the front door. 'Come on, Noah, be a love and put the kettle on, will you? I'm dying of thirst here. It's nearly half eight and we haven't had any bleeding dinner yet. And after the afternoon we had, I'm going to need at least four courses.'

Their time with the students had progressed from informative, to interesting, to traumatic, to eye-opening. After following Hunter up to his room, with resentment towards her radiating off him in bucketloads, they'd found a very peaceful Seth sitting up on the mattress on the floor, smiling as they'd entered the room. Shirley had tried hard not to stare at the red, raw ligature mark on his neck, she didn't want to be rude. But blimey, the boy had meant business, he'd really tried to properly hang himself by the look of things.

After initial introductions by Natalie, who had managed to procure another bottle of lager from somewhere on the way up all those stairs and was now finding it hard to stand up straight, Seth had said he was more than happy to talk to Shirley about Wednesday night. Despite Hunter's frequent attempts to shut him up, Seth had told Shirley about going off to find Eleanor after he'd left the bar. He'd said he was so angry and hurt, that he'd had such a go at her when he'd found her walking away from the ruined temple, that he'd made her cry, before storming off. And that, he'd said, was the last time he'd ever spoken to her, or seen her. He'd cried then, he obviously loved the girl. He'd explained how he'd smashed up his bedroom the next day, and the living room, and how he'd been arrested after his mum reported him to the police. He'd tried to hang himself in the police station, because at that time he'd truly believed that it was his fault Eleanor was dead. That because he'd had such a go at her, and called her names, she'd stumbled blindly off, fallen over, hit her head and died. But that, he'd said, was before he knew she might have been murdered. That changed things. Now he just wanted to find who did this to her, and kill them. Shirley had smiled at that point, because in her heart she believed Seth had been the most truthful of all the friends. His honest, upfront emotions were refreshing, although she did have to advise him against hurting anybody he believed had harmed Eleanor.

Natalie had chimed in at that point, saying that Hunter was carving a memorial for Eleanor out of wood, which was one of the reasons she'd decided to dump him that afternoon. She'd said he seemed to have time for everyone else except his own girlfriend. That he seemed to be actively avoiding spending time with her in favour of carving a bloody statue for a dead girl. Then Hunter had got angry, and shouted at Natalie, calling her an immature, selfish little cow, before turning and leaving the room, slamming the door behind him. When they'd finally got back into the car, complete with personal detail forms filled in by Natalie and Seth – Hunter had already stormed off by then – Shirley had decided to call in a favour with a friend who she used to work on club doors with, Paul Irving, and have police background checks done on everyone she'd spoken to so far. There was something bothering her about Hunter's behaviour, although she couldn't put her finger on exactly what it was. One thing was for sure, he *really* didn't want her sniffing around. Paul, her former colleague from her bouncer days – who'd gone into the police force at a similar time to her starting her own business – said he'd be happy to help, and that he'd phone her back when he had the information. At this stage, she had suspicions about all those kids. Hunter was acting strangely. Where had he really gone that night after leaving Natalie in the bar? And Natalie didn't seem at all bothered by Eleanor's death. Had even screwed her face up a couple of times when the girl's name was mentioned, she obviously hadn't liked her all that much for whatever reason. Alcohol – as Shirley knew all too well – tended to make you more honest than you normally would be. A memory of her telling Tiffany a few home truths one night after she'd drunk too much wine flitted into her head, and she quickly shook it away. No time for that now. Even Seth – he seemed to be telling the truth, but he had the biggest motive of all – his girlfriend had publicly chosen to spend time with another man over him, and it had obviously made him very angry. And Dillon – well. She intended to read his notes soon, and see what grains of information they provided – if any. All the people she'd spoken to seemed to be presenting one face to her and the outside world, that concealed the secrets they were harbouring on the inside. *My job here*, Shirley thought, *is to disentangle the actual truth from what they want me to believe is the truth. And I'm damn well going to do it.*

But first, she was going to enjoy a nice cup of tea, if Noah ever pulled his finger out and actually made her one, and read through all the papers and the notebook they'd recovered from Dillon's house.

'Thanks, Noah,' she said, as he walked forward with a full-to-the-brim cup of tea. 'Aren't you having some?'

'No.' Noah shook his head. 'Being in Dillon's house

reminded me how much I hate dust. I'm going to clean my room. I've put chips and burgers in the oven, they should be done in about half an hour.'

'Thanks,' Shirley said, smiling up at him. 'You know, Noah, I think I could get used to having you as my assistant. Can you just give me your notebook before you go up, so I can look over everything you wrote today?'

A few minutes later, Shirley had drunk half the mug of tea, and was opening the stack of notes entitled 'Eleanor' they'd found under Dillon's sofa. Her phone pinged, and she glanced at it. Good, it was an email from the trauma physician saying he could take a look at the head injuries on the autopsy. She looked back at the paper. What she read in the first paragraph made her eyes bulge and she sat back quickly, almost knocking the mug off the arm of the sofa.

33

'What a beautiful morning,' Marilla Parkhurst said, pouring her brother some tea. It was so hard to see Alistair completely broken like this. Emmeline's death had been bad enough all those years ago, and losing the use of his legs? Well, how on earth did one get over that happening? One minute you were a fit and active person, and the next you were confined to a wheelchair for the rest of your life. That whole horrendous episode had nearly killed him, but not quite, because he still had his shining star, Eleanor, to focus on. But now, he had nothing. Marilla was aware that she was probably the only person Alistair spoke to, now that Eleanor was gone. And she was finding it hard to even begin to lift his spirits, she didn't know where to start.

The Parkhursts were, on the whole, a very unemotional family. Marilla and her three brothers had been sent away to boarding schools as soon as they'd reached the age of seven, so all of them had quickly learned how to repress their emotions, how not to feel or miss anybody or anything. But Alistair's relationship with Eleanor had been different; he'd noticeably loved and cared for that girl. Probably making up for the affection he was missing in his marriage, Marilla had thought more than once. Now, seeing him slump over his breakfast plate, she was at a loss, she didn't know what to say. No point telling him to cheer up, that things would get better, because they wouldn't. And to say he had much to look forward to in life – well, he didn't. So she sat quietly, and hoped the day would go by quickly. She'd insisted on coming over on the Saturday morning, after talking to him on the phone the previous day. The tone of listless hopelessness in her brother's voice had been too much to bear, so she'd kissed her husband goodbye at half past eight that morning, and driven for an hour from her house in Cobham, Surrey, to be with Alistair in time for a late breakfast.

'I wish I hadn't hired her,' Alistair said, staring at his plate.

'Who?' Marilla asked.

'That detective woman, the one I told you about,' Alistair said. 'She wasn't at all what I was expecting, the information about her on the internet made her sound so professional. But when I met her, she was very common, rather rough. For all I know, she'll make off with the money I've given her, and I'll never see her again.'

'Ah,' Marilla said, glad to have a concrete, solvable problem to work with. 'Well, you know what you need to do then, Alistair, don't you? Phone the detective woman today, and ask for a progress report. If she doesn't give you a satisfactory one, give her a limited amount of time to improve things, and say if she doesn't give you results then you'll have to let her go. Then you can find a better one – Monty and I will help you, honestly, you should have asked us the first time round.'

Alistair brought his weary gaze up slowly to meet his sister's.

'Yes,' he said. 'I think you're right, Marilla. I'll phone her after breakfast. You should have seen her car, it looked like she'd just driven it out of a junkyard.'

'Good, Alistair, then you have a plan,' Marilla said with a small smile.

34

Declan Turner, a first-year biology student, was on his way to meet his friend Dean for an early morning game of tennis. The air was bright and fresh, the dullness of the last couple of days had gone, and as he rounded the corner of the main building, he breathed in deeply, enjoying the coldness. The tennis courts lay beyond the staff car park, and he made a beeline for them, cutting across the dewy grass, past a stone archway, and on past the pond where that poor girl was found dead – the area was still decorated with flowers – and round the side of the ruined temple.

That's strange, Declan thought, seeing the temple door open. Anyone who used it kept that door shut, to keep out wildlife and any other unwanted visitors. There was something on the ground, sticking out of the temple door. He took a few steps closer, then stopped dead in his tracks. It was a pair of shoes, covered in what looked like a lot of blood. Peering closer, a sudden ominous feeling that he didn't want to witness anything awful taking him over, Declan saw that the shoes were on the feet of a person, who was lying on the floor in a giant pool of dark-red blood. The person was most definitely dead. No one could have a pitchfork sticking out of their chest like that, and still be alive.

Turning away, a wave of nausea took Declan over and he bent down, unable to walk. The amount of stab wounds on the body was so frenzied, the face of the person was unrecognisable. But he was certain, from the shape, clothes and height of the body, that it was a man. Hauling his sports bag off his shoulder, he reached into the front pocket for his phone, dialling three nines.

'Hello?' Declan said when the operator answered. 'I need police at the Royal Buckingham University right now. Someone's been murdered.'

35

Detective Inspector Charles Linford took in the scene. As luck would have it, he'd been in Buckingham town when news of the murder had come crackling through his radio, and had arrived at the scene in less than five minutes. He'd seen many dead bodies in his time, he reflected, more than he could remember. He knew about cruelty, knew only too well what one human was capable of doing to another. But he was also aware this was going to be one job that stuck in his mind. The man in front of him had died a truly gruesome death; his gouged and bloody remains were testament to that. There were too many stab wounds for DI Linford to count by sight, and the killer hadn't been content with just these – whoever it was had also assaulted the victim's face with some sort of object until it was unrecognisable. The crowning touch was the pitchfork, still present, thrust deep into the victim's heart, amid some sort of tattoo. There was emotion involved here, some sort of dark passion. He would bet money that this victim had known his killer.

'Bad news,' he muttered, 'is exactly what we have here.' He was dedicated to his job; had given his life over to it for twenty-two years. And one thing he didn't like was getting things wrong. If truth be told, it didn't often happen. But as he stared at the mutilated body of the man on the ground, he was beginning to wonder about that girl Eleanor's death. Two deaths within a week at the same university campus – one definitely a murder? Now that was cause for thought. It was starting to seem regrettable that Eleanor's case had been dealt with so rapidly. Perhaps if more time had been taken, if a more thorough investigation had been conducted... well... But they'd all had their orders to reduce crime in and around Buckingham, hadn't they? The chief superintendent had been emphatic about it, uncompromising in his orders. No, there was no point wondering at this stage, DI Linford thought, bending down to inspect the body. Hindsight was always an exact science – as someone clever had once said – but foresight was most definitely not. Now, he had a job to do. There was no more time for reflection...

36

'Y ou fucking what?' Shirley said, rubbing her eyes.

'I said,' Noah repeated, 'get up, Shirley, there's been another murder at the university. I just heard them talking about it on the radio while I was eating my Shreddies.'

'Well I'll be buggered,' Shirley said, pushing the duvet off and swinging her legs over the side of the bed. 'Did they say who the victim was?'

Noah shook his head.

'What time is it?' Shirley looked at her phone. 'Ten to eleven. This is all we bloody need. This murder complicates our investigation, you mark my words, Noah. Right, we'll leave in five minutes, okay? The place will be swarming with coppers by now, but we need to go and have a look, too, while the scene's fresh. Not that they'll like it, but who cares. If you need to obsessively brush your teeth, for God's sake get on with it and don't keep me waiting.'

Seven minutes later, Shirley's Vauxhall Corsa was on its way to Buckingham. Her prediction, she found on arrival, had been correct; there were police cars parked at angles up the drive, and the grounds were swarming with high-vis jackets. Students had

151

flocked to the police tape blocking off a wide area around the ruined temple; their throng was abuzz with chatter and gossip. Two ambulances sat on the grassy area that was taped off.

'Such a shame it was Dillon,' she heard one of the girls say to her friend. 'I can't believe it. He was so fit, I really liked him. Who would want to hurt him?'

'Dillon,' Shirley breathed. 'It can't be. I was starting to think...' She stopped, and shook her head, then turned to Noah. 'I do believe we have a serial killer on our hands. And that is not good news at all. In fact, it makes things here rather dangerous. And it also makes our investigation much more complex, and in many ways we are back to bleeding square one.' A shot of fear, tinged with urgency, flooded her mind. It was now imperative that they found out the truth of what had happened to Eleanor as quickly as possible. If the two deaths were related, then it was likely that a third could happen at any moment, and Shirley wasn't sure she could stomach hearing about another dead body – three in a week was too much for anybody to digest.

'What makes you say that?' Noah said loudly. The girl and her friend turned round to look at him.

'Shh, keep your voice down, will you?' Shirley rolled her eyes. She stepped backwards, beckoning Noah to follow her. 'Christ, you're not exactly subtle, are you, sunshine? We don't want to advertise our presence here just yet. Private detectives don't have the same rights to investigate live crime scenes in the way that police detectives do; we're here on the down-low. We have to stay incognito. Our approach has to be more tactical, if you know what I mean. I say serial killer, because don't you think it's a bit of a coincidence that Eleanor and Dillon – the founder and a member of the Satanic Society, or whatever it's called – have been killed here within days of each other?'

'I suppose so,' Noah said. 'But I think we should let the

evidence speak for itself. Take a good look at all the facts, before we jump to any conclusions.'

'All right, MacGyver,' she said, a faint smile on her lips. 'You're absolutely correct, of course, as per usual. I was just sharing my initial hunch with you, that's all.'

She felt her phone vibrate in her pocket, and pulled it out. It was hard to see the screen in the daylight, but she could make out that the email sign was flashing. She pressed on it, and a message from the head-trauma expert appeared. Turning the phone this way and that, trying to read what she could in the glaring light, Shirley scanned the page of text. He'd already looked at the autopsy results, and other reports she'd sent him about Eleanor's death. *Quick work, my friend*, she thought. *Nice one.* She'd chuck him over the lump of money he'd requested by BACS when she got home. Eleanor's facial injuries, particularly the nasion haemorrhage, were indicative of intentional blunt-force trauma, the expert said. It was almost impossible to injure that region of the face by accidentally falling over. *Ha*, Shirley thought. *I knew it. I'll let Mr Parkhurst know ASAP that his hunch was right. Eleanor was attacked. Shame on the police for not conducting a more thorough investigation. Mind you, if they had, I might not have been given this job...*

'Shirley?' a man's voice called. She looked round and saw Paul, her bouncer friend from long ago, striding towards her in his police jacket. He was weightier than she remembered, and his hair was thinning on top, but other than that he was still her same old friend. 'All right, me old mucker?' He smiled. 'Long time no see.'

'Paul.' She grinned, despite the fresh wave of anxiety flooding her mind, giving him a quick hug. 'Good to see you, mate. I take it you're here working on Dillon's murder?'

'Blimey, secrets don't stay hidden for very long round here, do they?' he said with a chuckle, as he patted her back. 'Yes, that's why we're here. They won't let you see the body yet, if that's what you're hoping, Shirl. Probably for the best, that boy met a very grizzly end. There are so many stab wounds, all over his face and chest – plus a pitchfork lodged near his heart – that he's barely recognisable. Two university staff were able to confirm his identity from his hair and tattoos. If you ask me, it was someone who knew him and hated him that did this. That's usually the case when there's such a frenzied attack anyway.'

'Oh dear,' Shirley said, thinking of Dillon's beautiful face that she saw yesterday, and not wanting to imagine what it looked like now. What a waste of a person's life – even if he was a dodgy fucker. Murder was always abhorrent. Noah, she noticed, was staring at Paul, his face white, his mouth slightly open. *Poor boy*, Shirley thought, hoping her nephew wasn't going to faint. *I've thrown him right in at the deep end with this case. Oh well, can't be helped. If he's going to be a private detective he needs to toughen up a bit. It might be the making of him.* 'Any idea of the time of death?'

'From the state of the body, they think it was last night some time. Probably near midnight, or a few hours after,' Paul said. 'Obviously an autopsy will tell us more. Oh, by the way, I've got those background checks you asked for. Clearly Dillon's will be no use now, although I'll email it over anyway with the others. He's got quite a lot of previous, from a while ago. We've been watching him for some time. We were pretty sure he was dealing drugs in Buckingham, but we could never catch the crafty little bastard in the act, and no one wanted to snitch on him. Seth, as you probably know, was arrested for the first time the day after Eleanor's death, for smashing his mum's house up. Natalie's clean, but Hunter was the big surprise.'

'Oh really? Why?' Shirley asked. 'I thought something was off with him.'

'I can't explain now, I need to get back over there.' Paul gestured towards the crime scene. 'The DI's in a panic; I think he's probably wondering if Dillon's death is related to that girl, Eleanor's. Listen, I'll email all the reports over to you this afternoon, and you can take a good look at them in your own time. Okay?'

'Thanks, Paul,' Shirley said, patting his arm. 'You've really helped me out. I owe you one.'

'I'll hold you to that,' Paul shouted over his shoulder as he walked away.

'Shit,' Shirley said, a frown crossing her face.

'What is it?' Noah asked, a bit of colour returning to his cheeks.

'I read all of Dillon's notes about Eleanor last night,' Shirley said. 'To say they were fucked up is an understatement. He'd been watching her for weeks, back when she clearly had no idea who he was. He made notes about her clothes, what she ate and drank in the canteen, the make-up she wore, the friends she was with. It was beyond creepy. Even the times when she left the halls, and went back to them. He was spying on her, even before she joined his society. He was a voyeur, a sneaky spy.'

'Really?' Noah said.

'Yes.' Shirley nodded, turning to walk up to the main building. 'And he'd made detailed plans about what sex acts he would do with Eleanor, and the future times and places they would do them. It was so fucking predatory and controlling, it was unreal. Who's to say she even liked him in that way, anyway?'

'Well, from what her friends said yesterday, it sounds like she willingly stayed behind with him at the ruined temple,' Noah said. 'She wouldn't have done that if she didn't like him.'

'That's true,' Shirley said. 'But that's not the only thing. You know that notebook I took from Dillon's house? The one from the box under the sofa.'

Noah nodded.

'That contained even more fucked-up material.' Shirley shook her head as she plodded along. 'It was all about Satan and evil, and how the Devil is sending Dillon messages, telling him what to do. There were even prayers to Satan in it, it was so weird. I'm going to have to hand it over to the police.'

'Yes, you probably should do that,' Noah said.

'My point here is, Noah,' Shirley went on. 'That the evidence of Dillon being involved with Eleanor's death was mounting. The notes he made about her were sick, and I don't believe that tale he told us about Wednesday night for one minute – when he said Eleanor just stayed behind to help him tidy up the temple, and then went on her merry way. Something happened between them, I know it did. So either Eleanor's death was an accident, which seems more and more unlikely. Or Dillon did it, and there is another, different murderer on the loose who killed him. Or there is just one killer who finished them both off.' She sighed. 'Statistically, the third theory is probably the correct one. And we are still no closer to finding out who that killer may be.'

'That's not technically true, Shirley,' Noah said. 'Paul just said he's emailing you the background checks this afternoon. Maybe something in them will give you a clue.'

'Yes, I hope so, Noah,' Shirley said with a sigh. 'I could really do with one of those today.'

They stopped, having reached a door into the main building.

'Right, I'm going to find the head honcho, Professor Indigo Fielding,' Shirley said, setting her jaw. 'And I don't care if she is dealing with another death on her grounds. I don't care if she's having the busiest day of her life. I want to see in Eleanor's room right now. Today. No more excuses.'

37

Seth and Natalie were huddled together on Natalie's bed. Hunter had disappeared, locking his room before he went. They had no idea where he'd gone, and his phone was turned off.

'I can't believe someone killed Dillon,' Natalie said, her face white.

'I know,' Seth said. 'They might close the university for a while now, send all the students home. It doesn't feel safe here anymore.'

'No,' Natalie said. 'It doesn't.'

Seth shut his eyes.

'Dillon was so perfect,' Natalie said. 'I can't bear to think of what he looks like now.'

'Then don't,' Seth said. 'And he wasn't perfect. He just acted like he knew everything.'

'You didn't like him very much, did you? Not since Eleanor stayed behind with him at the ruined temple that night anyway?'

Seth sighed.

'No,' he said. 'I didn't. And I know I said I wanted to kill whoever hurt Eleanor. But I had nothing to do with Dillon's murder, Natalie. Okay?'

There was a pause.

'I believe you,' Natalie said. Then she looked down at her feet, and a tiny tear rolled down her cheek.

38

'I need to see Professor Fielding *now*,' Shirley was saying to a secretary whose mouth was in the process of puckering up tighter than a cat's arse. 'Right now. I need access to Eleanor's bedroom *today*.' She hadn't been surprised to see, on their way to the head honcho's office, that notices had already gone up around the university warning students to be extra vigilant, and to lock their rooms whenever they were in them. Go around in groups, the notices suggested. Stay inside after dark, if at all possible. If events carried on as they were, she wouldn't be surprised if they sent all the students home...

'Absolutely not,' the secretary said for the third time since Shirley and Noah had entered her office. 'Have you any idea of the chaos Professor Fielding is dealing with today, Ms Butterworth? Did you, by any chance, notice the plethora of police cars all over the campus? You can't come in here and demand things, especially on a day like this, when poor Professor Fielding has so much on her plate already.'

'Ah, but I'm not just demanding it today, am I?' Shirley said, her voice rising. 'I've been politely asking for access to Eleanor's room since Thursday. And today's Saturday. And I have one grieving father in Sussex who is counting on me for answers. And his daughter is dead, as dead as Dillon is out there. Now please, can I have the key to her room, Miss Whoever-you-are?'

'No, and you need to leave now,' the secretary said, lifting up the receiver of the phone on her desk. 'I don't want to have to call security...'

'Oh, for *fuck's sake*,' Shirley said, as an inner door to the office opened. An exquisitely poised lady with a shock of white hair entered the room. Her expression suggested that she was not feeling amused.

'Ah, Professor Fielding,' the secretary said. 'Ms Butterworth was just leaving.'

'No I wasn't,' Shirley said.

'I've been listening to this whole painful exchange,' Professor Fielding said, her voice surprisingly deep. 'And I believe now is the time for you to have the key to Eleanor's room, Miss Butterworth. Frankly, I have more pressing things to attend to today, than listen to this argument continue for one minute longer. I have the key here, and I will thank you to return it to me when you have finished. Patsy here will show you to Eleanor's room now.'

She passed the key to Shirley, then turned, disappearing back into the other room and closing the door.

Patsy looked like she would rather stick needles in her eyes than show Shirley where the room was, but her professionalism won through, and she walked off – haughtily, in Shirley's opinion – gesturing for Shirley and Noah to follow her.

Minutes later, the two of them were alone in Eleanor's room. Patsy had left without uttering a word, shutting the door a little louder than was necessary behind her. It was strange being in someone else's private space, Shirley mused, looking around. It felt intrusive, like you were spying on them. Even if they were deceased. But she was here now, and she had to make sure they had a thorough look at everything. She didn't want to miss anything at all that might give them a much-needed clue. Dillon's death, as she'd said to Noah earlier, put a much darker and more urgent frame on Eleanor's demise; if she was correct about a serial killer being on the loose then arguably everyone at the university was in danger. Only the police would have any weight with Professor Fielding in that regard, and she hoped they'd make it very clear to her how dangerous the campus now was. But Eleanor's death had been ruled an accident, hadn't it? She wasn't stupid, she'd heard on the news about Buckingham's rising crime rate. It wouldn't be the first time – in the history of lawbreaking – that an unexplained death had been ruled an accident so that the police could save face...

'Okay, Noah,' she said. 'Start going through those drawers over there, will you? Tell me if you find anything, and I mean *anything*, that could tell us more about Eleanor and what happened to her. Personal possessions, medication, photos, ID, writing of any sort, well, you get the picture.'

'Righto,' Noah said. Shirley turned away to look at the unmade bed, wondering what other seventeen-year-old boy in the world said 'righto'. The thick duvet, covered in a light pink case, was still turned back, as though the girl had just got out of bed. A fluffy dressing gown lay on top of it in a heap, and a vest top was thrown on top of that. Shirley sniffed; the room still had a faint whiff of the perfume Eleanor must have put on the night she went out. It felt sad, seeing her stuff lying around like this, a clothes hanger here, a lipstick there. Also, smelling her scent was very evocative. It made her more of a real person, as though she might walk back in at any minute. Shirley made a silent vow to the girl that she wouldn't stop investigating her death until she'd found out the absolute truth; of who had done this to her. Then she bent down, always a difficult task given her size, and peered under the bed. A sequined book lay there, just out of her reach.

'Here, Noah, get this book out from under here, will you?' Shirley said, turning. Noah nodded, and came over to retrieve it.

'It's Eleanor's diary,' Shirley said, thumbing through the pages. 'Look, she was good at art, there are so many doodles in here – stars, hearts and moons seem to have been her favourites. Ah, what's this?' she said, pointing to a scribble. 'It says, "Must phone Dad tonight, or he'll get upset again. But what else is there left to say to each other? We talk about the same things every time. Day after day. He is so co-dependent on me, I don't know what to do. He doesn't see me as a separate person from him. Why can't he just let me be free for once?"' She flicked over another few pages. 'End of October, and she's drawn a giant heart. Crikey, it's got the name Dillon written in tiny letters over and over again all around the edges. You were right, Noah. Looks like she did have feelings for the man after all.' She flicked the page over, then paused. 'Not just mild feelings either,' she said slowly. 'Eleanor was obsessed with Dillon, absolutely infatuated with him. I'm not going to read you some of the stuff she's written, Noah, because it might make your cheeks burn off. But take it from me, she was crackers about him. Well, at least we know whatever went on in the ruined temple that night was consensual. I was starting to worry about that after reading his disturbing notes...'

'Shirley, look,' Noah said. He was pulling some papers out of the top drawer of the desk. 'These might interest you.'

Shirley took the pile from him, and stared at the top sheet.

'*Dear Miss Parkhurst,*' she read. '*Thank you for your letter to West Sussex County Council's adoption agency. I understand that you are keen to trace the identity of your birth parents, and I have looked at all the information in your file. I regret to inform you that no names or contact details were left by your birth parents, they wished to* remain completely anonymous. I'm so sorry to give you this news, as I know you were hoping for a more positive lead. However, please be assured that I'm keeping your letter on file, and should either of your birth parents contact us with the view to getting to know you, we will have your details at hand, and will get in touch with you straight away.' Shirley shook her head, and handed the paper back to Noah. 'Poor girl,' she said. 'She was obviously desperate to find out more about her heritage.' As she was speaking, she absent-mindedly opened the diary on a page near the back. 'Look, Noah, this is apt.' She held up the page. Eleanor had written, *Who am I?* in the middle of the page, then surrounded it with question marks. Shirley stared hard at the words for a moment.

'I'm so stupid,' she said softly, shutting the diary and placing it on the bed. 'Why didn't I think of this before? Come on, Noah, there's something urgent we need to do.'

39

Eric Van Bern stared at the photo in front of him. Framed in silver, a tiny baby, just born, was lying swaddled in a Moses basket. He remembered the moment he'd first seen his daughter; she was so tiny, so fragile. But they couldn't have kept her – him and his then partner – they were both students at the time, so young, and far too immature. It had been his idea to give the baby away, he'd really had to persuade Francesca that it was the best thing to do for all three of them. They'd broken up soon after she was born, of course. The whole thing had weighed too heavily on them. He always kept the photo of her in his top drawer, liked to be close to it, but he hadn't looked at it for a while. Months, in fact. But everything had changed when Eleanor Parkhurst had started her master's at the university. All those feelings of grief, loss and confusion had resurfaced, and they'd been too much to bear. He opened the drawer and placed the photo frame carefully at the back of it again. This was his business, no one needed to know. Hardly anyone at work knew about the baby that he and Francesca had given up, all those years ago. It had been painful at the time, but this felt so much worse. Oh, why did that girl have to join *his* university? Of all the places she could have chosen. *Damn* her.

He let out a deep sigh, for everything that could have been, but wasn't, and would never be now. Then stood up, and walked over to the door, opening it. He caught sight of a flash of unruly ginger hair, belonging to a large bulk of a body at the end of the corridor, and quickly, quietly shut the door again. No, that woman Butterworth was the last person he wanted to see today. Nosy crow, snooping around his domain. She seemed incompetent; she had a general air of disorganisation about her, and hadn't exactly come across as professional with her style of interview. Mr Parkhurst had made a mistake when he hired that woman to investigate Eleanor's death. Goodness knows where the man had found her.

Eric was looking forward to the day when the university returned to its order and rhythm, longed for it, in fact. He couldn't stand all the disruption, the new people from the emergency services milling around who didn't belong there. It made the place feel messy and disorderly. And quite frankly, they were ruining the grounds with their heavy boots. He couldn't think properly with all the sirens blaring in and out; the whole thing was giving him a headache. Although with all the kerfuffle over Dillon's murder, goodness knows when peace will reign again, he thought. He walked over to the window, and stared out at the chaos in front of him, the flashing lights, police, tents, tape, and huddles of students.

40

Striding back towards the car, Shirley caught sight of a lone older woman, standing away from the throng. She was tall and thin, her shoulders were drooping slightly, her coat hanging limply around her. Her expression had a deadness about it, a defeat, a vacancy that was chilling. Her lined face was also strangely familiar. Propelled by instinct, Shirley approached her, offering a warm smile that went unnoticed.

'Hello there,' Shirley said, picking a patch of grass on which to stop, and planting her feet wide apart from each other. She felt Noah come to a halt next to her. 'Can I help you with anything?'

'What?' The woman turned towards her, her hollow, haunted stare finding Shirley's.

'Are you all right?' Shirley said. 'It's just that you seem a bit lost. I was wondering if I could help you at all?'

'I've come to see where my son died,' the woman said. 'Dillon Rushwell. Two police officers came to see me earlier, told me what had happened to him. I wanted to see for myself, as I didn't believe them.'

'Oh, I'm so sorry,' Shirley said. Her heart felt like it was breaking for the poor, crushed woman standing in front of her. 'I can't imagine how you must be feeling. How awful for you. Do you want me to ask if you can come closer to the crime scene?'

'No.' Dillon's mother shook her head. 'I can see enough from here. I know it's real now, he's truly gone. I hadn't seen Dillon for six years, you know?' She turned towards Shirley. 'I can't say I liked my son that much, not after how he behaved, what he did. Isn't that awful? I'm here, looking at the spot where he was murdered, and I'm telling you I didn't even like him.'

Her eyes filled with tears, but they didn't fall – just sat in the rim of her eyes, forming tiny lagoons.

'No, it's not awful, it's honest.' Shirley wanted to reach out and hug the woman, but didn't know if she should. 'We all reach limits, all have boundaries round what we are prepared to put up with.'

'The drugs made him so much worse.' Dillon's mother shook her head, dislodging a trail of tears. 'He always had trouble telling fantasy from reality, you know? Everything got muddled up for him, and that made it confusing for me. I never knew where I was, what he'd be like when he came home. But when he started smoking marijuana, and then went on to take stronger stuff, he became almost evil. It was like he was possessed. He robbed things from me so many times, and sold them to get drug money. I have no jewellery left now, other than the cheap stuff my husband's bought me since. He pretty much tortured his sisters with insults and threats, telling them he would punish them if they didn't give him what he wanted. They were scared of him. Started staying away at their friends' houses a lot. The last straw was when he held a knife against my throat one evening, said Satan was talking to him, and that any minute he might be told to finish me off so that I could learn my lessons in Hell. That was it, I had to put my other children first, you know? I chucked him out. Told him not to come back. And he didn't. I haven't heard from him since.'

Shirley nodded.

'We'd tried to get Dillon help many times,' his mother went on. 'But he was a good actor, he changed whenever a professional was interviewing him, started acting normal again. It was like he had multiple personalities, you know? Could just switch them around whenever he felt like it. He never showed the psychiatrists his true colours. It was like he could switch the evil on and off at will.'

'That must have been terrifying for you all,' Shirley said. It made her glad that Noah was so square, hearing all this. Her nephew might be an oddball, but he was a lovely one. And he'd never hurt a fly, let alone steal from or threaten an actual human.

'It was.' The woman nodded. 'I was scared for my life, in the end. For all our lives. His father was useless, he's a weak man. Never helped me with the children. He left it all to me to deal with, and I never really knew if Dillon had it in him to actually hurt us badly physically, but I didn't want to leave it too late to find out.'

'I understand,' Shirley said. 'It sounds like you made the right decision.'

'But I'll never see him again now.' Dillon's mother turned back to the crime scene. 'And I never stopped loving him, all this time. The love got weaker and more difficult, but it's always been there. It always will be. I don't think any mother in their right mind can ever truly stop loving their own child. Dillon was a lovely boy when he was little, you know? So inquisitive and bright. Into everything, a real live wire. His teacher in primary school said he was hyperactive, but his behaviour never bothered me, not at that stage. It was nice to see him running around and climbing trees all the time. But everything changed when he was about eleven. Some sort of darkness took him over then. I felt I was losing him, and now I really have. And I'll have to live with the fact that I threw my own son out of my house, that I couldn't help him, for the rest of my life.'

'No, you can't think like that.' Shirley shook her head. 'You did the best you could at the time. You couldn't have done any more. Don't punish yourself with that kind of talk.'

'Well, I'll never know now, will I?' Dillon's mother said.

Shirley followed the woman's gaze to the chaos by the temple. She didn't envy her one jot; it was clear her existence would be bleak from now on, as she constantly wondered whether she should or could have done things differently with her son, whether she was in some way to blame for his demise. Of course, she wasn't, she did what she could to help him. But that kind of guilt could be all-consuming, she suspected.

'No,' she said quietly. 'But like I said, you did the best you could.'

41

Shirley was pulling the seat belt around her enormous girth when her phone sprang into life, the *Star Wars* ringtone filling up the car.

'Oh, who the bloody hell is this?' Shirley grabbed the device and stared at it. Damn, she'd been hoping to go and look up some information; it was urgent she found out if her hunch was correct – because if it was, it could turn her whole investigation on its head. 'Oh, it's Mr Parkhurst. I better answer it or he might get the hump.'

Several minutes later, her face pale, she gently laid the handset down on the dashboard, and stared straight ahead at the rain sprinkling across the windscreen.

'Well, that didn't sound like it went very well,' Noah said from the passenger seat, retrieving an apple from his coat pocket.

'No, not particularly.'

'What was Mr Parkhurst actually going on about?' Noah said, shining the apple with his sleeve. 'I only caught bits of it. He sounded cross.'

'Basically,' Shirley said with a sigh, 'I think he's regretting hiring me for this case. He wanted to know what firm evidence we've found. As you heard, I reminded him he only contacted us two days ago, and that we would need a bit more time before I could present him with anything concrete. I tried to tell him about hiring the traumatic head injury expert I'm in touch with, and that the man has already confirmed that Eleanor's head injuries are inconsistent with an accidental fall. In fact, they actually indicate foul play, especially the nasion one. I said we finally got access to Eleanor's room, and found some good leads there, and that we've interviewed members of staff and Eleanor's friends, and have several good ideas of how to go forward, but he wasn't listening properly, he kept interrupting. It was like he didn't want to hear what I had to say.'

She looked down at the steering wheel, a heavy feeling of worry and sadness pervading her. For fuck's sake. Why was this happening? She'd been putting so much hard work into the case every day, had been feeling really driven to carry on and see it through to the end. She felt a connection with Eleanor now, she thought. And on a personal note, she wasn't ready to give up yet. After all, she'd made a promise to the girl in her bedroom, hadn't she? And Shirley was never one to break a promise if she could help it. Even so, Mr Parkhurst's words had hurt so much it was like he'd physically struck her. He was withdrawing his trust in her capabilities, but that trust had meant everything – it had bolstered her in ways she hadn't realised until now.

'This case is so important to me, Noah,' she said, angry that her voice was thickening with emotion. Fuck it, she wasn't going to cry. 'It meant so much that he'd entrusted this to me, I really thought things were looking up, and that I had you to thank for that – after you advertised Justice Investigations across social media and everything. And, of course, the payments he promised would set us up for the next year. But it was about more than the money, it was about someone believing in my abilities, it really sounded like he did when I first spoke to him on the phone. But when we went down to Sussex to meet him, something must have put him off. Probably me. I've always known I'm more like Marmite than jam to people, you know? I'm big, I'm loud, and some people are prejudiced against ginger hair. But mostly they hate common accents and dented cars, especially if they're posh. And let's face it, my car's a shit bucket.'

'Shirley,' Noah said, chewing. 'You have to remember what you told me in the student bar the other night. You said, "It's important never to give a, er, fudge, about what other people think of you. Especially if they're being judgemental". I think you need to take your own advice now, don't you?'

'Yeah, I know.' Shirley stared hard at the horn on the steering wheel. 'But sometimes it's not that easy, especially when people have not believed in you and your business for so many years. Especially your family. And then this ray of hope comes, when someone trusts you with a big job. It's even worse when they take it away, it hurts more than if you'd never taken the job on.'

'I think you're being melodramatic, Shirley,' Noah said. 'Mr Parkhurst hasn't taken the job away from you. He's just threatened to – from what I could hear. And I believe in your business. I asked to join it, didn't I?'

'You're the exception, my love.' Shirley reached over to pat his knee. 'And I'm very glad you are. Anyway, you're right. Mr Parkhurst has said we've got until Wednesday midday. And if we don't come up with some solid answers for him by then, then he's taking us off the case and hiring a new private detective.' She struggled to keep her face composed. Mr Parkhurst had struck her where it hurt, she knew. Just when she'd thought they were doing a damn good job, and starting to get lots of leads. Fuck, she'd actually been enjoying herself. She'd felt her confidence rising day by day, and she'd begun to really like working with Noah too. The boy was useful, he took rather good notes, even if he had become obsessed with directly transcribing her speech. Now she felt like she'd been kicked in the guts. Like she'd failed.

Noah shrugged.

'Well, that's okay then,' he said. 'That's four days, if you include the rest of today. Lots of time. Don't worry, Shirley, it will all work out. We'll just have to work even harder.'

Shirley sighed.

'Listen, Noah, I need some time to think about our next move now,' she said, turning towards him. 'Have you still got the names of Eleanor's classmates that Professor Weatherby gave us?'

Noah nodded.

'If I leave you here at the university by yourself for a couple of hours, do you think you could do some sleuthing on your own?' Shirley said. 'I'm giving you a chance to be independent here, an opportunity to strike out on your own in the business for the first time. You know, get some proper investigating experience. It would be really helpful if you could find as many people on that list as possible, and ask them about Eleanor? How well they knew her? If they know anything about her movements on Wednesday night?' She watched his facial expression change as he considered this proposition. She tried to ignore the niggle in her brain that was telling her it might be dangerous for Noah to go back there by himself, what with a serial killer on the prowl and everything. She loved her nephew – despite his oddities – and would never forgive herself if anything happened to him. But she needed some time by herself so badly. After all, he didn't like people in general, so would keep out of everyone's way wherever possible, including the murderer's. So it was worth a shot. Socialising practically gave him a rash. And he was probably stressing about wanting to brush his teeth, which seemed to be his usual response to imminent public engagement. She wasn't holding her breath. But if she could just have a couple of hours to herself...

'Fine,' Noah said. His breathing had picked up, Shirley noticed, and he was now fidgeting with his seat belt. 'But only for two hours, okay, Shirley? Don't leave me here longer than that.'

'Ah, well done, mate.' Shirley slapped his knee. 'You're a star. Fantastic. We're on a fucking time limit now so the more work we can cover as a team the better. The more we can work on different things at the same time, the faster we'll get this job done. We need to get some answers ASAP. Out you get then. Make sure you've got your notebook, pen and that list, that's it. Have you got your phone with you?'

Noah nodded.

'Great, I'll give you a ring when I'm on the way back.' Shirley watched him exit the car and close the door. She gave him a wave, watched him walk off, then turned her head away and let the tears fall down her cheeks. Why did Mr Parkhurst have to go and say all that? she thought. Why did he have to lose confidence in her so bloody quickly? It wasn't fair. His words had stung, really hurt. She turned the key, and the car sprang into life. Knowing exactly where she was heading, and that she needed to get away from the university and those two deaths for a while, she revved the gas, turned towards the exit and kept driving.

42

'Ah, Daniel.' Eric Van Bern walked faster to catch up with his colleague. 'Has that awful woman gone yet, do you know?' The bare electric light was buzzing loudly above his head, and he glanced up at it, annoyed.

'Who, the private detective?' Daniel said, turning and suppressing a smile. 'I'm not sure, Eric. I haven't seen her today, I didn't know she was on campus again.'

'She's always here nowadays,' Eric said, as they rounded the corner into the stairwell. 'Making a lot of fuss about nothing, if you ask me. If the police say Eleanor's death was an accident, why can't the family just accept it?'

'It must be hard for Eleanor's father, I imagine,' Daniel said as they trotted down the stairs. 'It must be horrific to lose your daughter, accident or not. People always want someone to blame when tragedies happen. Maybe that's got something to do with it.'

'Yes,' Eric said. 'Maybe you're right. Do you have the time? I need to get to that pastoral meeting.'

Daniel shifted his sleeve up, then shook his head.

'No, sorry,' he said. 'I'm not wearing my watch today and my phone's in my office.'

Eric nodded, and turned to walk away, but then turned back suddenly.

'Oh, bad news about that chap Dillon, eh?' he said. 'I'm finding it hard to stomach another death at the university, especially so soon after the other one. And it's turned the grounds into a police circus. Flashing lights and emergency workers everywhere. I can't think in my office, there's too much commotion. Bring back a bit of normality, I say.'

'Yes.' Daniel paused, looking at his colleague. 'And I'm wondering if the police will now change their minds about the manner of Eleanor's death, maybe open up another investigation into it. Apparently, Dillon's demise was particularly unpleasant, and they might wonder at the coincidence of two deaths so close together here.'

'In some ways I hope they do investigate Eleanor's death again,' Eric said as he started to walk away. 'Anything's better than that Shirley Butterworth woman; she's so coarse, it makes my skin scrawl.'

'Yes,' Daniel said, blinking. 'Perhaps.'

43

Shirley drove blindly down to Buckingham town, with rain splattering against her windscreen, then kept going up the A422 towards Milton Keynes, straight over the roundabout near Old Stratford and onwards towards Northampton. She needed to be near water, she thought, remembering her childhood holidays at Southend. Not just the bloody rain, she needed to see a stretch of water, like a lake or a river. The endless beaches and grey-blue sea had always felt like a welcome balm and break from her dysfunctional home life. She'd always looked forward to those times. Once, when her dad had been having a two-day reprieve from chronic depression, he'd sat on the sand with her and they'd built castles and dug moats together. Then the tide had come in and gently washed water through the channels, before its endless energy drove waves to swamp their entire masterpiece. It was a halcyon day, the two of them together, at least that's how she remembered it now.

Spotting the grey waters of the canal to her left, and a sign for Stoke Bruerne, Shirley did a sharp left-hand turn off the main road. She was in a country lane now, driving past fields, hedges and sheep. A few minutes later she'd parked up and was walking south down the bank of the Grand Union Canal. Past the pretty café and rental houses that overlooked that stretch of water, past locks, pubs and dog walkers. On and on, until she was away from everyone. The canal banks were more unkempt here, less manicured. The only living things she could hear were the birds tweeting in the trees, calling to each other. Occasionally she passed a moored narrow boat, but all of them sat silently in the water, as though any passengers realised she didn't want distractions. The sight of the murky water – raindrops bouncing off its surface – was just as soothing as she'd known it would be; it was almost as though it could absorb her stress. Act as a sponge for anxiety. Further on she went, the water just a foot away from her on her right-hand side, past a lone fisherman, an abandoned Coke can, a heron on the opposite bank. Finally, a ray of peace shone through her broken mind. It was like soothing mental balm. *Ah*, she thought with a sigh. *That's the ticket, keep it coming.* She was still pissed off, still hurt and angry. But the wave of out-of-control angst had broken, she could feel it. Now she might be able to talk some sense into herself. But actually, perhaps not. She'd lost all motivation to carry on pretending to be a functional adult.

All she wanted to do right now, she realised, was drink a bottle of red wine. Or four. Maybe five. She could actually taste it in her mouth, taste the firm, fruity flavour. She'd been secretly proud that she hadn't gone out and bought more, when Noah – bless him – had hidden her stash. But now, fuck it. What was the point? If Alistair Parkhurst took her off the case, there would be no kudos in the private investigator world for her. There would be no good review, no word-of-mouth praise, nothing. He was going to fucking fire her for sure, she knew he was. She could tell from his withering tone that he'd already made up his mind. He'd probably already started looking for a replacement... She stomped further along the canal path, barely registering the trees and undergrowth she passed. The rain had stopped, but the clouds were still low and grey. She'd done her best on this case so far, she really had. And she'd been pleased, felt like they were getting somewhere, even if she didn't have all the answers yet. But now, she felt like her enthusiasm for it had been extinguished. Or crushed, more like. Posh git. Who did he think he was, judging her like that? She kicked a large twig out of her way. This was bad. No, not just bad, it was a fucking disaster.

As usual, when she was feeling down, all the other sources of hurt in her life sprang into life in her brain. Tiffany, her beloved girlfriend had left her. Just walked out. She was so useless she couldn't even keep a relationship going, let alone a business, she thought. She'd thought Tiffany was the one, for a while at least. Thought they'd live out their days together. But no, it hadn't happened. She was alone once again. No one believed in her work, not even her family. No one, except Noah. She was such a fucking loser; why the hell was she even bothering to try in life? Why not just give up now? Get a whole crate of wine and be done with it. She imagined the addictive, wonderful oblivion of drunkenness taking her over, washing away her hurt and pain. It would be so easy, all she needed to do was buy a few bottles and go home. Noah would make his way back eventually...

Are you really going to let Alistair Parkhurst destroy your confidence like this? a small voice said at the back of her head. *Are you going to let one old man take you down like this? I thought you were stronger than that. What happened to big, bad, invincible Shirley?* Shut up, she thought to herself. Stupid fucking conscience trying to give her a pep talk. But she had a point. Was she going to head back to Winslow, go straight to the off-licence, buy their entire stock of Yellow Tail Merlot, and spend the rest of the evening getting more wasted than she'd ever been before? She imagined the look of disappointment on Noah's face when he eventually found her slumped over and unconscious. But bloody hell, she would enjoy getting into that state. She would revel in every mouthful, celebrate the opening of each bottle. Or was she going to go and try to find Eleanor's birth parents as she'd planned to, when she'd been standing there in the poor girl's bedroom? Eleanor might not have accessed those records successfully herself, but as a private detective, Shirley would, her plan had been to make sure of it. And a hunch was telling her to look at them. That a vital clue would be found, if she looked in the right place. Which course of action would she choose? she wondered, stopping and turning to look at the sludge-green canal water. A thin shaft of sunlight slithered through the clouds and illuminated a patch near a lock. Alcoholism or perseverance? She honestly didn't know the answer right now. It was a very tough choice. Oh well, better head back to the car and find out...

44

Shirley banged open her front door, threw her bag on the sofa, then kicked the door shut with a slam. Shit. She'd said no to alcohol. It felt weird; she wasn't sure she'd ever done that before. Not voluntarily, anyway. Driving past the off-licence had been extremely fucking hard; she'd been so tempted to stop and buy wine. A lot of it. She could almost smell the rows of beautiful bottles from her car. Imagine them clinking away on the drive home, then standing there all gorgeous and straight on her coffee table, with a nice large wine glass ready and waiting in front of them. Getting drunk was an old habit, she knew, and it worked for her. Up to a point. Actually, it only worked for a few hours, but still, they were a few very happy hours. But in the grand scheme of things, she knew deep down that alcohol would destroy her life in the end, if she didn't get a grip on her addiction. Yes, smart-arse Noah was right, damn him, she was a fucking alcoholic. It was a family trait to be fucked up in one way or another. But no more time for naval-gazing now, she thought, picking up her laptop, before sitting down. There was work that needed doing.

Remembering Paul's promise to email through the

background checks he'd done on Eleanor's friends, she leaned over and quickly fished her phone from her bag, then stared at the screen. Would he have remembered? She couldn't really blame him if not, it had been chaos for the officers up at the uni. Yes, the good old boy had done it, a message from him was flashing up. Seconds later, she was opening the attachment titled 'Hunter McPherson'. He was the one she was most interested in, so far his behaviour had been more than suspicious.

'*Hunter McPherson – also known as Thomas McPherson – holds one criminal conviction for rape,*' she read. *Does he now?* she thought. *That's extremely interesting.* Maybe her hunch about the adoption records had been wrong... '*On the 4th July, McPherson was tried at Reading Crown Court for the rape of nineteen-year-old student, Jacqueline West.*' *Ah, the case went to a crown court*, Shirley thought. *It might have attracted media attention, I'll have a look in a minute.* '*The jury concluded that West did not consent to have sexual intercourse with McPherson, and he was convicted of the offence of rape, receiving a seven-year sentence. He was released from Woodhill Prison in Milton Keynes after serving five years.*'

Well, well, well, Shirley thought, quickly searching up news reports of the case on her phone. *Hunter – or should I say Thomas – you* do *have a secret to hide then. One that may take this case in a whole new direction.* She clicked on a link, and brought up a *Daily Newsflash* page emblazoned with the title: *Man Rapes Drunken Student After Offering to Walk Her Home.* She scrolled down to the opening paragraph. '*Thomas McPherson, who also goes by the name Hunter,*' she read, '*has been convicted of raping his friend, Jacqueline West, after offering to walk her home after a boozy night out. The two were part of a larger group of students who had attended the Cat Club in Reading Town Centre. After complaining that she was feeling sick, West accepted McPherson's offer to walk her back to her student accommodation. She admits to being very drunk that night, and says once home she fell into a deep sleep on her bed. McPherson, who had reportedly been obsessed with West for some time, decided to have sex with her. When she woke up the next morning, he informed her about what he'd done, and the horrified West immediately went to the police. A rape test confirmed the presence of McPherson's DNA in West's body. Officers arrested McPherson later that afternoon. West says the attack has left her traumatised, and has suspended her studies for six months.'*

Interesting, Shirley mused, as she put her phone down. Could Hunter really be responsible for Eleanor's death? And possibly Dillon's too? After all, he had connections with both of them. And his movements were unaccounted for that night, after he'd left Natalie in the student bar. And he had a history of violence against women... She needed to speak to him again, as a matter of urgency. He'd suddenly become a very strong candidate for the job of murderer.

But first, she had more research to do. Opening her laptop, she quickly brought up the MyForebears site, opened the birth index and put in Eleanor's name and the date she was born. It was a trick she'd learned during her private investigator training; use the ancestry sites for their records, her tutor had said. They're a goldmine. She rapidly scanned the six pages of results. No hits. Which probably meant that Eleanor was not the name the birth parents had given their daughter. Bugger, she'd forgotten to ask Mr Parkhurst about that. And she didn't fancy ringing him now, not after the earful he'd doled out just before. She cleared the search, and typed in a new name. Eric Van Bern. If her hunch was right...

Twenty-six records came up, a mixture of Van Berns and Erics, but she couldn't yet see any with the first and last name together. She scrolled through them, looking for any that stood out and grabbed her attention. Ah, here was a hopeful one, she thought. She clicked on it. She stared at the results. Lucy Imogen

Van Bern, mother's name Francesca Larkin, father's name Eric Van Bern. Shirley took her hand away from the screen, and stared. It wasn't hard to work out that from the date of birth shown, Lucy Imogen Van Bern would now be twenty-two. The same age as Eleanor was when she'd died. She'd have to check the date of birth was the same as Eleanor's, but then it wasn't inconceivable that that had been changed too. Not the first time it would have happened. And Noah had all the bloody notes with him. Was Lucy the daughter Professor Weatherby had been referring to when he spoke about Van Bern giving away his child? Surely it was too much of a coincidence, that twenty-two-year-old Eleanor, who'd been adopted, had started at the same university as her biological father – apparently without knowing the connection between them – only to be killed?

Hang on, slow down, Shirl, she thought to herself, her heart racing. *This is a good lead, a bloody great one, in fact. But don't jump to conclusions just yet. You need to investigate Hunter, or Thomas or whatever his frigging name is, and find out what he was up to on the night of Eleanor's death. He's a very strong candidate for the killer right now. But still... this information is hot as mustard. Van Bern's a strong suspect too. I need to phone Mr Parkhurst right now and find out if he knows what Eleanor's birth name was. I know he said it was a closed adoption, but you never know...*

She picked up her phone, and clicked on his name. The ringing tone went on for what seemed like ages, but Mr Parkhurst didn't pick up. *Damn,* she thought. *Now what?*

Her phone bleeped as a text came through. Looking down she saw it was from Noah. *Oops,* she thought. *Forgot about him for a while. I should really go and find him at the university, see whether those students have eaten him alive or not. God knows how long it's been since I left him...*

She brought up his message. 'I managed to find two of Eleanor's classmates,' she read. 'Their names are Ebony and

Murphy. Murphy was really friendly, he told me that their other classmate, Ciara, isn't on campus at the moment as she's gone home to see her parents. Murphy said he liked Eleanor, that she was a friendly, chatty classmate. He was out late in town with a group of friends the night she was killed, then stayed over at his girlfriend's house. He said Eleanor was probably the smartest in their class, but thought it was strange that their tutor, Daniel was the hardest on her, yet gave her the most attention. Apparently he was always demanding more from her, but also asked her the most questions, which Murphy thought was odd, but was probably because Daniel is such a slave driver. Ebony wasn't very friendly towards me, she didn't want to answer many questions, but she did say that Eleanor was all right, although a bit too flirty with the boys sometimes. She didn't want to speak much after that, so I left the main building and went outside. Can you come and get me now, Shirley, please? I don't want to be here by myself any longer. I'll wait for you in the visitors' car park.'

Bless Noah, Shirley thought, throwing her phone back in her bag, before standing up. He'd done well, considering he hated talking to most human beings in general. And he'd given her a chance to regroup, to think about things, clear her head a bit. And she was pleased she'd chosen the sober way forward for once, hard as it had been. Well, she had two strong leads now, Van Bern and Hunter. Now all she needed to do was to find the bastards and talk to them again. Noah wouldn't be pleased, but when she got to the university they would need to stay there a while longer, and hope that her two main suspects were still around on campus somewhere...

45

Something was bothering Seth. There was a detail bugging him about the night that Eleanor died; he'd remembered that he'd seen a person hanging around the grounds that had surprised him because that person shouldn't have been there then. The memory had unexpectedly flitted back into his head as he was drinking a cup of tea about half an hour ago. He remembered feeling surprised when he'd seen them, but only fleetingly, as he'd been too angry with Eleanor that night to care much about anything else. His lack of recall wasn't surprising really, he thought, given how hammered he'd got after the New Satanism session – he'd drunk a lot in the bar with Hunter and Natalie, started doing shots – tequila and Jagerbombs, if he remembered rightly – when he'd realised Eleanor wasn't turning up to meet them. But the alcohol increase hadn't really helped, as it turned out. Had just made him more and more angry. But there was no point in kicking himself over that anymore, he thought. What was done, was done. The only thing he could do now was remember as many details from that night as he could...

Who was it? Who had he seen? *Think, Seth, think.* It might be important. Or it might not be. He wouldn't know until he could recall who he'd seen there, near Eleanor, in the dark. He turned over on his mattress, the one he and Natalie had nicked from an empty student room and put on the floor of hers. He'd now moved in with her, managing to retrieve his belongings from Hunter's room when the man had briefly returned from wherever he'd been. He'd gone somewhere again now, disappeared off the campus. He was acting strangely, and it was freaking Seth out a bit. His friend had completely shut him out, and wasn't talking to him or Natalie. It was like he'd closed down, become an isolated island of a person, which was making Seth concerned. Why would Hunter act like this? It couldn't just be because Natalie had broken up with him. He'd started going weird after that detective lady had turned up and spoken to them. For some reason, her presence at the university seemed to make Hunter nervous, panicked almost, and very angry.

Natalie, on the other hand, was turning out to be a much better friend to him at the moment. He'd never really got to know her before, she'd always just been Hunter's girlfriend, someone who was always around but who he rarely properly spoke to. But she was being very kind to him; she knew he didn't have much money and was always bringing him food and drinks, and she was funny, too, had a really dry sense of humour. He wondered why he'd never noticed this before; maybe because she generally seemed quite shy and overshadowed in a group? The only downside, of course, was that she didn't own a PlayStation, but strangely, he hadn't had much of an urge to play on one since leaving the hospital...

Okay, go back through that awful night step by step, he told himself. *Try and remember who you saw out in the grounds. It might mean nothing, but it might mean something. And you need to find out who did this to Eleanor, so think, man.* He remembered stumbling away from the student bar and across the lawn. It had been a freezing night, he remembered, the sky pitch black, a very far away moon casting only the faintest light across the grounds. All the statues, arches, ruins and other decorative architecture had just appeared like black blobs in front of him. He'd met Eleanor as she was walking away from the ruined temple; she hadn't looked at all happy, but that hadn't stopped him from giving her both barrels of his hurt and fury. He felt ashamed about that. Then he'd turned and walked away, spotting someone familiar to his left as he'd stormed off. That person hadn't seen him, he wasn't facing towards him, but Seth had recognised the person easily and been surprised that they were there. It was...

He sat up as the memory flooded through his mind. He now knew exactly who he'd seen that night. No wonder he'd been surprised to see them out and about in the university grounds late at night. He reached for his wallet, and took out the card that lady detective had given him. She'd said to give her a ring if he remembered any other details from Wednesday night, no matter how small. This may mean nothing, but he was going to tell her about it anyway, just in case.

46

———

Hunter walked through Tingewick Woods in the darkening gloom, his axe hanging from his hand. It had taken him over an hour to walk from Buckingham, his watch informed him, but he hadn't noticed the time passing. All he'd felt – as he'd walked purposefully out of the town and along the main road – was the air on his cheeks, and the pain in his mind. A couple of times he'd wondered if a truck or van would hit him. He wouldn't have minded. He wasn't like Seth, didn't have those suicidal thoughts. But an accidental ending to his pain, now there was a notion that brought welcome relief.

Now, his eyes were staring straight ahead, although he wasn't taking in much of the view in front of him. He hardly saw the shadowy, bleak, bare trees, the mess of undergrowth on the floor, the occasional fallen branch and the swirls of dead leaves. He'd had to get out of the university, there had been no question about it. The walls had been closing in on him; he'd felt so trapped in his room, so claustrophobic in there, especially after that fucking detective woman had come sniffing around.

How much did she know about his past? Did private

investigators have the same access to criminal records as police? He had no idea. But what he did know was that he was going mad. Doubting himself, hating everyone around him. Unable to look after Seth anymore, and feeling rejected by Natalie. And Eleanor and Dillon were dead. Hunter's living hours had taken on the tinge of a nightmare, and it was scaring him. His thoughts hurt, they kept whirling uncontrollably around his mind, taunting him.

The events of Wednesday night were now a jumble in his mind. He'd seen Eleanor, he knew that. He remembered speaking to her after he'd left the bar. She'd been upset, and she'd smelled of booze, which was unlike her. But when he tried to remember what happened next, after that, his thoughts became disordered, fractured. Memories of what he'd done all those years ago to that girl were now mixed in with recollections from Wednesday night. He'd dreamt about Eleanor for two nights running now, when he had managed to drop off into an exhausting sleep. In one of the dreams he was smashing something into her face. Was that a dream, or had it actually happened? He wasn't sure. He must be losing it. Going mad.

But there was no way he was going back to prison. He couldn't, it would kill him, he was certain of that. But he could sense that it was going to happen. Flashbacks of the day of his trial, all those years ago, the verdict being read out, then being led away to years of incarceration, kept playing through his head like a film reel stuck on repeat. He needed a way out...

On and on he went, tramping over twigs that snapped, and dead leaves that crackled. No one else was about, which is what he wanted. No dog walkers, no hikers. It was probably too cold for them. But the icy air was nice; it was the only thing that was good in his life right now. It smelled of freedom. Right now, he needed to be very far away from everyone, from every living thing. He didn't actually want to hurt anybody, he never had. But it had happened anyway…

He stopped and looked around. He was lost now, had no idea which direction was which, or how to get back to the main road. Perfect. He lifted up his axe, and brought it down in front of him with all his might.

47

───────

Daniel walked out of Professor Fielding's office, closing the door quietly behind him. Well, that was a very satisfactory outcome, he thought. A few weeks of much deserved leave had been arranged; he rarely took time off his work for anything, but was currently feeling the need for a break. Events had been full-on recently, what with one thing and another, and he needed time away to think.

He hitched his sleeve up to look at his watch, but then remembered it was broken and lying on his bedside table at home. Damn, he couldn't find that silver buckle anywhere. The watch was an antique; his father would turn in his grave if he knew it was damaged; it had originally belonged to his grandfather. No matter, he would fix it in due course.

Making his way along the corridor towards his study, he was surprised to see the now familiar shock of red hair appearing round the corner, followed by the rest of Shirley Butterworth. That drip of a boy was following her.

'Hey,' Shirley said, her voice loud. 'Have you seen Professor Van Bern anywhere? I need to talk to him again. It's important.'

'Er, no I haven't, sorry.' Daniel stopped and shook his head.

'Perhaps he's in a meeting? Although it's getting a bit late for that now. Maybe he's already gone home.'

'Shit,' Shirley said quietly, before turning and walking off again. 'Come on, Noah, look lively, we've got to find the man.'

Daniel stroked his chin as he watched her go.

48

Seth tried Shirley's number again, but it just rang and rang before going to voicemail. He put his phone back in his pocket as he walked down the hall corridor. If he couldn't get through to the detective, he'd have to go and find the person he'd seen that night, he decided. Ask them some questions, see if they knew anything about what had happened to Eleanor. They probably didn't, but it was worth a shot.

Passing a window, he saw the remaining police presence in the grounds, left behind to continue the investigation into Dillon's murder. It was dark outside now, was sometime past six. Lights had been erected around the white tent the police had erected at the ruined temple, and he could see several Day-Glo jackets still there, as well as plain-clothes officers and a forensic team wearing white protective suits. A shiver of fear ran through him and he turned his head away, immediately catching sight of a hastily put up poster warning students to look after themselves. To only go out in groups. To lock their bedroom doors at night. Someone very dangerous was still on the loose, and he knew he was putting himself in danger by trying to find out who it was. But he owed it to Eleanor, still knew in his heart

– no matter what other people said – that if he'd looked after her that night instead of shouting and being angry, that she'd probably still be alive.

Working his way through the web of corridors in the old building, he finally arrived on the floor where the faculty of art had their offices. Now, which was the right door?

49

————

'No, I can't stay here any longer, I'm afraid,' Eric Van Bern was saying to Shirley through the half-wound-down window of his red Chevrolet Corvette C8. His eyebrows were lowered and drawn together, and his eyes were hard as they stared at her. 'I don't care if there's more you need to ask me. No, I'm sorry; it's Saturday evening, this has been a very trying day, and I have someone I need to meet. Even us academics are allowed some of the weekend to relax, you know. Now move out of the way.'

'But Professor Van Bern,' Shirley said loudly, as the car started to reverse. 'I just need to know about your daughter, Lucy. Do you know where she is now, Professor? Have you seen her recently? It would be very helpful to my enquiry if you could just answer me before you go.'

'Look,' Van Bern said, his face a contortion of anger, slamming his foot on the brake. 'I know exactly what you're getting at, Miss Butterworth, and I'm afraid you have got it all wrong. Anyway, why are you so obsessed with my past? I'm not the only member of staff at the university who has given their child up for adoption, you know. Are you harassing Daniel

196

Weatherby about his child too? Or have your great detective skills not led you to find out about his private life? Look, I can tell you categorically, neither Daniel nor I had anything to do with Eleanor's death, or with Dillon's either. So if you want to actually do something useful, go and bother a real criminal for a change.'

Van Bern reversed the Chevrolet at speed, turned, then drove away into the darkness. Shirley's mouth was open. Her hand went to her head and she turned to Noah, who was wrapping his arms around himself.

'Oh fuck,' she said. 'I've been a blind idiot, Noah. The truth was right in front of me all the time. Oh fuckity fuck. Wait, I need to look something up quickly.' Why the hell had it taken her so long to work this out? Jesus Christ, was she a bleeding detective or wasn't she? She was always bemoaning others for only looking at the surface of people, for taking them on face value, and now it turned out she'd been doing exactly the same thing herself, stupid cow that she was.

She quickly reached into her pocket for her phone and brought up the MyForebears site again with a few taps, opening the birth index and typing in the name Daniel Weatherby, and Eleanor's date of birth. A result immediately sprang onto her screen, and she opened it. 'Chloe Grace Weatherby. Father Daniel Weatherby'. Born twenty-two years ago.

'Shit,' she said, turning towards the main building. 'Come on, Noah, we have to find this man right now.'

'Why, what's happening?' Noah jogged to keep up with her. Shirley ignored him, turning on her voicemail as she walked. Seth's voice came to life, telling her he'd just remembered something, a detail about the night Eleanor died. He said that he'd seen Professor Weatherby out in the grounds late on Wednesday night. It had surprised him to see the professor there so late, he said. It was unusual because most of the academic staff didn't live on the campus, they always went back to their homes after lectures and tutorials finished. Then he said that as he wasn't able to get through to Shirley and kept getting her voicemail, he was on his way to find the professor, to see if he knew anything about Eleanor's death that might be helpful.

'Fuck,' Shirley shouted, as she broke into a run.

50

'In you go,' Daniel said to Seth, as he opened the front door to his cottage. 'I'll just go and get the photographs of Eleanor for you. I know how much they'll mean to you.'

He locked the door from the inside, slipping the key into his pocket. Why did this little rat of a boy have to go sticking his nose into things that didn't concern him? Daniel had been surprised to learn that Seth had seen him on Wednesday night. It had annoyed him; after all, he'd been so careful. He'd known Dillon had seen him out in the grounds, and it had given him pleasure to take care of that slimy piece of work, who thought he was such a big man. Of course, he'd had to do it slightly earlier than planned – after that Satanic weirdo had come looking for him, trying to blackmail him about seeing him out near the pond on Wednesday night. Dillon would never have been good enough for Eleanor, *never*. It was a joke that he'd thought he was even in with a chance. Now, how was he going to make Seth's imminent death look like a suicide?

'Make yourself comfortable,' Daniel called over his shoulder, as he walked away, motioning to Seth to go into the living room. 'I'll be back in a second.' He made his way to his bedroom, thinking hard. What would be the best way to kill Seth? The boy already had a reputation for attempted suicide, if he used his brain he could avoid all suspicion, everyone would believe Seth had just succeeded this time.

But first, he could have a little fun with the boy. After all, he wouldn't be going anywhere now. Well, he'd promised Seth photographs of Eleanor, hadn't he? Lured him away from the university with that little carrot. He'd show him some photos all right, but they wouldn't be ones Seth would be expecting...

51

Shirley heaved herself up and over the top step, and rounded the corner into the domain of the faculty of arts, Noah at her heels. The corridor was empty, and very quiet. No sounds of life and business could be heard, no coughs, muttering or printers whirring from behind the closed doors. She found Weatherby's study door, knocked hard and waited. There was no sound from inside. She grabbed the handle, twisted and pushed. The door was locked. Damn, fuck and bugger, she'd been too late. The man must have already gone.

'Someone's coming,' Noah said, and Shirley turned. Could it be him?

A petite girl was walking down the corridor towards them.

'Can I help you?' she said as she approached. 'Are you looking for someone?'

'Yes, we're looking for Professor Weatherby,' Shirley said, aware that her voice was coming out in harsh, fast bursts. 'Have you seen him at all?'

'He's already gone, I'm afraid,' the girl said. 'I came to hand my essay in to him about half an hour ago, and he was just on the way out. He was just about to give a student a lift somewhere. I've been working in a research room since then, and I haven't seen anyone else about.'

Oh God, Shirley thought. *Please say it's not...*

'Er, do you happen to know the name of the student he was leaving with?' she said.

'Yeah, I think his name is Seth,' the girl said. 'He's the one who tried to kill himself the other day. His neck looks awful, so red. I couldn't stop looking at it.'

'Thank you,' Shirley said. Her heart felt like it was plummeting down through the floor. She was too late. 'You don't happen to know where they were going, do you?'

'I'm not sure.' The girl raised her eyebrows, obviously taken aback by all the questions. 'I overheard Professor Weatherby saying he was going to give Seth some photos or something.'

'Thank you.' Shirley turned and started running back towards the stairwell. 'Come on, Noah, we need to move fast. Follow me.'

52

Seth was feeling uneasy. He was perched on the edge of Professor Weatherby's sofa, waiting for the promised photos of Eleanor. But something didn't feel right. He shouldn't have come, he'd known that as soon as he'd got in the car and the central locking had clicked into place. In fact, he'd gone to see Professor Weatherby to try and find out if he'd harmed Eleanor in any way, although when he'd got there he'd been stuck for words. The man had been so polite to him, it had thrown him off course. God knows why he would want to harm Eleanor anyway, she'd just been his student. What possible motive could he have had? She'd never even liked her tutor, was always saying how strict and tough he was. But when the professor had said he had some lovely photos of Eleanor he could give Seth, taken when she was giving art presentations, he'd been too tempted, and had agreed to go with him. He was so stupid, he knew, he'd let his heart get the better of him. But the idea of having actual photographs he could frame and look at, rather than the few selfies of the two of them that he had on his phone, had been too irresistible. His stupid phone that would have been very useful right now, but that had gone and

203

run out of battery. He was aware that no one knew where he was. Why hadn't he let someone know he was going with the professor?

Now, sitting in the quiet cottage, that was detached and isolated in a village near Buckingham, Seth had a bad feeling. He couldn't fully explain it. He was listening hard for sounds of Professor Weatherby coming back with the photos, but could hear nothing. He stood up and walked out of the living room. The front door was just there in front of him, and he tried the handle. The door was locked. Very firmly. And he couldn't see a key anywhere. Fear and panic were rising fast within him now. What did this mean? Why had Professor Weatherby locked him in like this? And where had he disappeared to? Why wasn't he coming back?

53

———

Shirley reversed the car out of the university car park faster than a rally driver, then turned and accelerated off down the long drive.

'Are you sure you have all the forms with you, Noah?' she said. 'The ones we got all the interviewees to fill in?'

'Yes, of course I do.' Noah was reaching round to the back seat and pulling a folder towards himself. 'I always bring this wherever we go. Just in case.'

'Please remind me,' Shirley said, 'to never take the piss out of your amazing organisational habits again. Okay?'

'Sure,' Noah said. 'But I'm certain you will anyway.'

'Come on then,' Shirley said, as they swung on to the main road that led into Buckingham town. 'Get Weatherby's form out and tell me the address, will you? I don't even know if I'm heading in the right bloody direction at the moment.' Adrenaline was coursing through her veins; she wanted to speed through the town centre but the bloody traffic was as bad as usual. Her palms were sweaty, they were slipping on the steering wheel. Christ, why had it taken her so long to suspect Weatherby? she wondered for the umpteenth time in the last five minutes. The bleeding murders had nothing to do with frigging Satanism, they were to do with the age-old motives: passion and revenge.

'Hang on.' Noah retrieved a sheaf of papers from the folder, and thumbed through them. 'Ah, yes, here it is. The address is Mill Cottage, Bridge Lane, Thornborough.' His voice was quavering a bit, Shirley noticed. *Poor sod must be as nervous as I am.*

'That's just up the road.' Shirley checked her mirrors, then pressed the accelerator down harder, then braked as she nearly drove into the back of another car. 'You know, that village about three miles from Buckingham, towards Milton Keynes? We'll try there first. If Weatherby said he was going to give Noah some photos, and didn't have them with him in his office, so had to give him a lift somewhere, it makes sense that they've gone to the man's house.'

'Well,' Noah said. 'Let's hope he's given you the right address. If it is him who's been murdering people, he may well not have.'

'Yep, that's true.' Shirley nodded. 'But it's the best information we've got. Listen, pull my phone out of my pocket, will you, Noah? I want you to phone Paul, you know, my friend who's in the police now. Just scroll down till you find his number. I want you to tell him everything we know about Weatherby, and that he has a student called Seth with him, whose life is probably in danger right now. Tell him he's already killed two people so there'll be nothing to stop him doing it a third time. Oh, and Noah? Ask Paul to check we've got the right address for Weatherby, will you?'

54

As Daniel walked back into the living room, a bag slung over his shoulder and several photo folders in his hands, he saw Seth pacing from one side of it to the other.

'Are you all right?' he asked with a smile. 'You look a bit, I don't know, nervous?' The boy's breathing was shallow; he seemed terrified. As well he might be.

'I need to leave now,' Seth said, his words coming out in a rush. 'I've just remembered I'm supposed to meet someone. They'll be wondering where I am. Can you let me out, please, Professor Weatherby? Don't worry about giving me a lift, I can make my own way there. Just open the front door and I won't bother you any longer.'

'Oh, don't rush off.' Daniel sat down on the sofa, and patted the seat next to him. 'Come and join me. I've just gone to the trouble of finding these photos, at least let me show you some of them?'

Seth hesitated, then slowly sat down, as far away from him as possible. His face was pale, and his hands were shaking, Daniel noticed. He reached behind himself and pulled the curtains tighter shut.

'Don't want any nosy neighbours looking in, do we?' he said, opening a packet. 'Now, let's start with these.' He handed the pile to Seth, then sat back, ready to observe the boy's reaction.

Seth looked at the first photo, his eyes wide and staring.

'I thought you said they would be of Eleanor giving modern art presentations?' he said, his face white. 'Why are you showing me this? It looks like Eleanor didn't know you were taking it.' He looked down again.

Daniel leaned over, and gazed at the image of Eleanor walking up a path towards the university. He'd taken it from his car, while sitting in the staff car park. He'd enjoyed watching his daughter like that, knew almost all of her movements; where she went, who she went with, the bars and clubs she'd attended, and, of course, the time she'd spent at that ridiculous society in the ruined temple. It had given him a thrill. He was always careful, of course, always took pains to stay incognito. It wasn't hard, she would never have suspected what he was doing, so there was no reason for her to be on the lookout. He was the silent watcher, the observer of his stunning, sensual child.

Seth was checking through the whole pile of photos, his hands shaking.

'Why have you done this?' he said, looking up at Daniel. 'You took all of these without Eleanor knowing. Like you were spying on her. What kind of sick weirdo are you?'

Daniel smiled slowly.

'Isn't a father allowed to photograph his own daughter?' he said.

55

As Shirley pulled into the road that led to Thornborough village, she cursed the lack of street lighting. Why did the countryside have to be so fucking dark? It was like driving blind, her car headlights only reached so far – only shone on the crumbling tarmac, and ghostly trees and bushes within a few feet. The high beams and fog lights didn't illuminate much more. It was a thick, black, freezing night. And the clutch of fear, of dread at what they would find at Daniel's house, had a firm grip on her body now. She couldn't afford for it to become paralysing; she had to keep a clear head, and somehow calm down. She could hear that Noah's breathing was getting faster and faster next to her. This was a new situation for them both; she'd never investigated a murder before, and Noah had never been out on any case before at all. Talk about being thrown in at the deep end. She had to look after her nephew; show him she was competent to lead him into whatever nightmare they were going to encounter. His trust in her was touching to the point of being overwhelming, Shirley thought, and she wasn't about to let him down.

'It's left at the end of this road,' Noah said breathily, staring at the live directions on his phone. 'Then straight on for a while, through the main part of the village.'

'Thanks,' Shirley said, as she swung the steering wheel round. There wouldn't be another murder tonight, she thought, no way. Not if she had anything to do with it. She suspected – knew in her bones actually – that Weatherby had killed Dillon too. And the only motive she could think of was that Dillon had seen something suspicious that night. But why was the man doing this? Why kill his own daughter? It just didn't make sense. But she knew she was going to find out soon, one way or another.

'Second right,' Noah said. His voice was louder than usual. Shirley sneaked a look at him – his eyes were bright and very wide, as though every ounce of focus in his body was shining through them. 'At least Paul confirmed it's the correct address. Do you think the police will be there when we arrive, Shirley?'

'I bloody hope so,' Shirley said, feeling a strong spike of adrenaline rush through her. *Good, keep it coming*, she thought. *Adrenaline will help counteract the fear.* 'I hope they're taking what you told Paul seriously, Noah, and actually deploy some officers. But if not, we'll think of something. Okay, so now where?'

'The house should be down near the bottom of this road,' Noah said, staring at his phone. 'Mill Cottage.'

Shirley nodded, thinking how isolated it felt to be out in the darkness like this. They were well out of the village now, and had just driven past a turning to a farm, but other than that there were no houses, no signs of human life around them. And the ghostly, dark view through the windscreen was reminding her more and more of a horror film...

56

'Leave me alone,' Seth yelled. His arms were up, ready to fight. If this sick fuck thought he was going to harm him, he was mistaken. He hadn't survived the suicide attempt on Thursday only to give in to death today.

'You can shout all you want; no one's going to hear you,' Daniel said with a sick smile. Seth wanted to kick his face, smash the smugness out of him. He watched the man reach round to his bag and take out a piece of long, thick rope. 'Now be a good boy and let me get on with this, will you?' Daniel said. 'It's what you want to happen, after all. You tried to kill yourself the other day, didn't you? Just think of this as me helping you to finish the job. Why not relax and enjoy it.'

'No,' Seth shouted, his voice harsh. 'I don't want to die, you fucking crazy psycho.' Daniel had backed him into a corner of the living room. He was running the rope slowly through his hands. His face had changed; he was no longer the hard-working art tutor that everyone at the university knew, he was evil, a monster – it was written all over him. Dillon had thought he was bad, but he'd been nothing but deluded compared to the person in front of him right now. This man, this psycho

Weatherby, was truly wicked. He was clearly enjoying Seth's fear; feeding on it like a mosquito feeds on blood. Smiling and chuckling. And what he'd said about Eleanor being his daughter? What the actual fuck had that been all about? No time to think about that now...

Seth glanced at the rope being moved around in Daniel's hands. He'd nearly vomited when he'd first seen it; had known exactly what it was meant for. The mark on his neck still burned from when he'd tried to hang himself in the police station. But that was then, and this is now, he thought. *I've changed. And I don't want to die, not anymore. But I do want to get justice for Eleanor. So get a grip, come on. Do whatever it takes to stay alive. Fight for your fucking life, man.*

He ducked as Daniel lunged at him, trying to hook the rope around his neck. He reached his hand out quickly, tried to grab the rope to pull it away, but the man was too quick for him, grabbing it away out of his reach.

'Come on, play ball,' Daniel said. Seth saw that he was no longer smiling. His eyebrows were getting lower and his upper lip was curling back. 'It won't take long, I promise. Be a good boy now.' He tried to throw the rope round Seth's neck again, then again and again, over and over, but each time Seth ducked and darted away from the psycho's reach. And each time, when he tried to grab on to the rope and pull it away, he missed.

Daniel, his face now ugly and contorted, his eyes looking blacker and more insane than before, threw the rope behind him and lunged forward.

'That's fine, we'll do this the easy way, shall we, Seth?' he said, hissing the words through his teeth. 'You little bastard. You really thought you were good enough for my daughter, did you? You're a piece of shit, Seth. A nobody, who will be better off dead. No one will miss you. No one will mourn you. In fact, they'll barely notice you're gone. She was too beautiful and perfect for you, my Eleanor. Too perfect for anyone. Except me.'

Seth coughed as Daniel's hands closed around his neck. He tried pulling away, kicking, struggling, but the man was too strong. He could feel the hands squeezing tighter and tighter, restricting his air flow. He grabbed the hands and tried to pull them off, tried putting every last ounce of strength into it, but Daniel was more powerful than he looked and held fast. A screaming panic overtook Seth and he knew there was nothing else he could do, he was losing the strength to fight. He was going to die right there and then, and then the murdering psycho that was Daniel Weatherby was going to make his death look like suicide. He scratched the top of the monster's hands as hard as he could, before the choking became too much. He let go. He had to, had no choice. He had no air left in his lungs, he couldn't breathe in or out. This was it; his last experience on earth. Seth's eyes closed as a delirious blackness overtook him.

57

There were no police waiting for them when they'd arrived at Mill Cottage. It had been a silly thing to hope for really, Shirley thought, unrealistic, as they would have seen a police car – or heard one – while they were driving through Thornborough. There were several ways in and out of the village, but it wasn't a large area, and police cars weren't exactly subtle vehicles, were they? A renewed panic rose in her throat, constricting it. They got out of the car anyway, on her instructions. What else could they do? Seth was in heinous danger, and she wasn't about to abandon him. But she needed her brain to work in double-quick time, to tell her what to do next, and so far it hadn't come up with anything. And she was well aware that she needed to keep her nephew safe.

'I can't hear anything, can you?' Shirley whispered. They'd made their way to the side of the cottage, creeping like cats in the dark. Noah's face was eerily white in the thin beam of pale moonlight shining on him. Someone was in the house, she was sure of it; there was a car in the driveway, and she could see chinks of light shining through the edges of the ground-floor window's tightly shut curtains. Would they have heard her car pulling up? she wondered. She'd turned off all her lights before they'd arrived – parked outside in the road – crept on to the drive as quietly as they could. But even so – who knew what Daniel would have heard, or even where he was right now. Perhaps he was outside? She looked around, but saw nothing but Noah, the house, the lawn and driveway, shadows and moonlight.

Noah shook his head.

'No. Shouldn't we wait until the police get here?' he said. 'Before we do anything? Paul said they would be on their way.'

Shirley looked at him, uncertain about the best way forward. He was so trusting, had full faith in the mechanisms of authority, as though everyone would reliably arrive on time when they were expected to. Her instinct was telling her to barge the front door, or smash through a window, and find Seth. To hell with the consequences. The thought of another young person dying at the hands of Weatherby was too much to deal with, especially when she was standing right outside his cottage. So close, but unable to help, to see what was going on. But Noah wasn't tough, he was the opposite, in fact. She looked at him. If anything happened to him, her sister Gloria would actually kill her. Literally. With her bare hands. She opened her mouth to reply, but at that moment a noise made her look round. There'd been some sort of thump from inside the building. God only knew what was happening in there. Nanoseconds after she'd heard it, the sky above them filled with wailing sirens. Shirley turned and saw blue lights flashing through the hedge. Thank fuck for that.

She turned back to Noah. But he was no longer there.

'Noah?' she called as armed police officers approached her. 'Come back here now, do you hear me?'

But Noah didn't re-emerge. Where the fucking hell had he gone? Surely he hadn't gone round the back? What if Daniel had got him...

58

Shirley was literally shaking as an armed officer shouted, 'Police! Open the door!' Whoever was in there, Weatherby or Seth, or even poor Noah – she couldn't bear to think of it – they, clearly weren't planning on coming out of the house voluntarily.

She had been about to tell Noah to go and sit in her car, to put the central locking on. He'd helped her enough on the case, pulled his weight with all the interviewing and note-taking, and she didn't want him getting hurt. But now he'd disappeared.

'My nephew,' she tried to tell the nearest officer, but he wouldn't look at her. Her mouth was so dry she could hardly talk. 'I need to find Noah. Please help me.' But no one was listening.

Just then, there was a crunching sound on the gravel and Noah appeared round the side of the house. Shirley's heart did a leap while at the same time a whoosh of anger rushed through her. She reached out and whacked his head.

'You little...' she said. 'Jesus Christ, Noah. Where the fuck did you go? I was about to have a God damn heart attack. I thought...'

'So you do care about me after all,' Noah said, a smile playing on his lips. A police officer turned round and glared at them.

'Be quiet,' he said through gritted teeth. Shirley glared at her nephew one more time, but kept her mouth shut. *There'll be plenty of time to ask him what the hell he was just playing at later,* she thought. *Little shit. Giving me the fright of my life like that.*

There was no sound from inside the cottage. No sign of movement. The front door stayed firmly shut. Why wasn't Seth calling for help? she wondered. What had happened to him? *Oh Christ, please let him still be alive. Please can that fucking maniac not have taken his life too.* A dizziness had overtaken her brain; *don't faint, you lightweight,* she commanded herself. *You have to stick this one out. Stay strong, woman.*

'Police!' the officer shouted again. 'Open the door. This is your last chance, or we're coming in.'

Still nothing. No movement, no key turning in the lock.

Then chaos kicked off. An officer smashed through the door with a battering ram, and a line of armed officers entered. There was shouting, and she heard a violent struggle going on inside. Men were yelling, but she couldn't tell if any belonged to Seth or Weatherby. After what seemed like ages, there was a lull, and an officer came out to announce to his superior that the scene had been neutralised; that Weatherby was handcuffed and restrained.

'I've got a pulse,' a man's voice shouted from inside. 'On the young man's body. It's very faint though. Are the paramedics nearly here?'

Two days later...

59

Shirley stared out of the grimy window of Tucker's café, watching the traffic grind to a halt down Buckingham High Street. *The traffic light system here is nuts,* she mused. *The town centre is nearly always gridlocked.* But she loved the place, enjoyed the energy and quirkiness that the students brought to it. Had always marvelled at the number of coffee houses and charity shops that lined the street, as though they were all residents of the town needed to get by. It all worked, it was vibrant, in a way. And now that Weatherby had been locked away it was a safer place than it had been two days ago.

A sound made her look up, and she saw Paul place a steaming mug of coffee on the table in front of her.

'There you go, old bean,' he said, sitting down opposite her.

'Thanks, Paul,' Shirley said with a smile.

'No worries,' he said. 'You can buy me one next time. Anyway, I was glad you rang – you've got me out of a few hours of shopping with the wife. She's after a new lampshade for our bedroom. Has to be lime green, apparently. God knows why. Can you imagine anything more boring than looking for one of them for ages?'

Shirley laughed and shook her head.

'Right,' Paul went on. 'I expect you'd like to hear what's been happening with that nasty bastard, Weatherby?'

Shirley nodded.

'Yes,' she said, her smile quickly disappearing. 'I know you're not supposed to tell me any of this, Paul, and I really do appreciate it. I won't even tell Noah, I promise. I'll keep everything you say completely confidential. It will just do my own mind good to understand what the fuck he did all this for, you know? I just really need to try and understand his motive.'

Paul stared at her for a moment, then nodded.

'I've always trusted you, Shirl,' he said. 'And I know you're as good as your word, no worries about that. Anyway, you're practically one of us – we're all working towards the same end goal, aren't we? And, at the end of the day, I think you have a right to know, given the amount of work you put into the case. Well, Weatherby was a tough nut to crack, I can tell you. He didn't talk easily. But we wore him down, and presented him with all the evidence against him. Eventually he knew the game was up, and that there was nothing to lose by talking to us. Then once he'd started he didn't stop; it was like he was proud of what he'd done, he wanted to boast, to show off his crimes.'

'So what was his motive for killing his own daughter?' Shirley leaned forwards. 'I've been racking my brain, but nothing seems to make sense.'

Paul sighed.

'Listen,' he said. 'The details aren't nice, but here we go. Basically, it turns out that Weatherby had fallen in love, or lust, with his own daughter when she started at the university. He didn't initially know she was his, the daughter he and his then girlfriend had given up for adoption all those years ago. He just thought she was a beautiful young student who happened to be in his master's class. But he began to put two and two together when Eleanor told him she was adopted; and he saw something familiar in her – apparently she looks like his sister did when she was younger. Anyway, he did some research – he's good at that, being an academic – and found he was definitely Eleanor's father.'

'Blimey,' Shirley said. 'That must have made him feel a bit weird.'

'Yes, you'd think so wouldn't you?' Paul said. He stopped and shook his head. 'In actual fact, it seemed to make Weatherby's feelings for Eleanor grow even stronger. It's a phenomenon apparently, called genetic sexual attraction. Not many people know about it, and it's very taboo, but it's a real thing. One or both relatives, who haven't met before for some reason like adoption, can feel massively attracted to each other when they first get to know one another, for some reason. It's rare but it happens. Anyway, Weatherby became obsessed with his daughter, started stalking her, taking photographs of her that she never knew about. You should have seen the amount that we recovered from his house; he'd obviously spent hours of surveillance on her.'

'Okay, that's weird,' Shirley said slowly. 'Everything you said just now is melting my brain as I try to process it.'

'It gets worse,' Paul said. 'We recovered video tapes, too, of him – ah – pleasuring himself as he watched videos of her giving student presentations. He'd recorded himself doing it. Sick bastard.'

'Oh God.' Shirley closed her eyes. *How am I ever going to tell Mr Parkhurst that?* she wondered. *Or actually, maybe I won't. There's no need. The poor man's been through enough, and passing on that vile detail won't aid him in any way. In fact, knowing about it would probably destroy him for good. I won't make things worse for him than they already are, poor sod.*

'But why did he do it?' she said, opening her eyes again. 'Why murder Eleanor? What was the point?'

'Well, it took us a while to get that bit of information out of him,' Paul said with a sigh, picking up his mug. 'But eventually he told us that he'd become so obsessed with his daughter, so consumed with feelings of lust for her, that he felt if he couldn't have her, then nobody could. He felt consumed with jealousy just at the thought of her having a boyfriend. Apparently seeing her become distracted by text messages in his class, and not concentrating on her work was the last straw. Seth wasn't much of a threat when he was dating Eleanor, as Weatherby suspected she wasn't that into him. But from his surveillance of her, he knew she'd just started going to the New Satanism Society, and rightly suspected the object of her desires was Dillon. He knew this man already had a much tighter grasp on Eleanor's emotions than Seth ever would. He couldn't handle it, and decided he had to kill her.'

'So killing her was better and more acceptable than being in love or lust with her?' Shirley said, feeling a red-hot anger rise through her body. 'What the fuck was he thinking? Why not just get a job somewhere else? Or take a break for a year until Eleanor had finished her course? Or even discuss his feelings with her and explain he could no longer be her tutor?'

Paul paused.

'The thing is, Shirl,' he said. 'When sociopaths kill, it's usually about control. Weatherby had restricted himself from actually sexually touching his daughter in any way, for some reason he'd given himself that boundary. Fantasising about her and stalking her was all right to him, as she had no idea how he actually felt. But acting out on his feelings would be a violation, to him. Killing her made sense to him, as he stopped anyone else from having her. It's skewed logic, but then murderous motives generally don't make a lot of sense to the rest of us. And he took an enormous amount of pleasure in murdering Dillon – it seems. Not only was Dillon the only person Weatherby knew had seen him out in the grounds that Wednesday night, he also rightly believed he was his love rival, that Dillon had a grip on Eleanor's affections. We know – from evidence found in Eleanor's room yesterday – that this is true. That's why he destroyed Dillon's face like he did. It was a crime of passion. And he planted the pitchfork in his chest to try and confuse investigators, make it look as though the murder was Satanic-related. He said he bought the pitchfork on an internet site in advance, after he'd decided what he was going to do – since he knew Dillon had seen him. He tried to kill Seth merely because he found out that Seth had seen him out and about in the grounds on Wednesday night. Weatherby said his plan was to strangle Seth with the rope, then take him back to the university in the middle of the night, and hang him off a branch of a tree in the grounds using the same rope. He would have got away with it if it hadn't been for you realising about his adopted daughter at the time you did. And the sad thing is, because Seth tried to hang himself after Eleanor died, everyone would have presumed he'd done it to himself again, but succeeded this time.'

'I see.' Shirley exhaled. 'What an utterly evil git.' She was quiet for a moment. They both sipped their drinks. Looking back on it, she could see that the signs that the murderer was Weatherby were there: the silver buckle that she and Noah had found in the pond where Eleanor died – Paul had phoned her yesterday to say it had come off Weatherby's antique watch when he was attacking his daughter. He'd asked her to bring it straight to the station. Also, he'd been quite keen to tell her about Van Bern's adopted child, hadn't he? She hadn't realised at the time that he was diverting attention from himself, had just thought he was being helpful, dozy cow that she was. And Weatherby had been quite happy to point the finger of suspicion at Dillon, hadn't he? Told her he wasn't trustworthy, or honest. Which Dillon wasn't. But Weatherby was worse.

'And Van Bern?' she said after a while. 'I started to think he was a strong suspect. Bit weird, isn't it? That he and Weatherby gave up daughters for adoption at around the same time?'

Paul nodded.

'Yes, it's weird, Shirl, but that sort of thing happens,' he said. 'I've been in this job long enough to have seen many strange and weird coincidences that don't make sense. But that's just life, you know? Sometimes it doesn't make sense.'

Shirley nodded.

'Yep, I guess you're right,' she said. 'Van Bern's shiftiness must have been partly because he's one of those freaky oddball academic types, and partly because he had given up a daughter for adoption who was the same age as Eleanor. Maybe the girl's death touched him, you know? Made him realise what he'd lost? And perhaps he knew he'd be under suspicion, once I realised he'd given away his child. Hunter was another one, what with his dark skeletons in the closet. But do you know what, Paul?'

'What?'

'I was so bleeding certain, initially, that Eleanor's death, and then Dillon's, must have something to do with Satanism,' Shirley said with a sigh. 'It just seemed such an extreme society, so out of the ordinary, with such a bad reputation. I leant too fast towards it being involved in some way. I should have been more objective, and let the evidence take me wherever it needed to. Silly bastard that I am.' She'd had to contact Lucifer Johnson, head of the Satanic Temple, the day before to cancel their imminent meeting. Which had been a shame, as she'd been kind of looking forward to meeting him. The tenets of the Temple of Satan had really piqued her interest when she'd researched them, she had to admit. They just made so much more sense than any other type of religious waffle she'd encountered. Maybe one day she'd join the movement – or religion, or whatever the fuck it was. Mainly just to infuriate her mum, who'd no doubt have kittens if she found out her daughter was a Satanist. She considered the notion for two point three seconds. Then, *nah*, she thought. *I don't answer to anyone except myself. And occasionally Noah, when he's in the middle of a cleaning frenzy. And anyway, Devil horns wouldn't suit me... they'd clash with the colour of my hair...*

Paul smiled.

'But that's exactly what you did do, in the end, Shirl,' he said. 'Can't you see? You were the one who actually solved this case. We just turned up at the end and arrested Weatherby. Dillon thought he was clever, he thought he could control people, lead several different lives like some sort of Machiavellian character. But in truth, he was just a messed up and disturbed young man. We know, from the evidence we recovered from his house, that he thought he was being controlled by Satan, which I highly suspect was something to do with the large amount of skunk we also found. My colleague did some research into it and says that actually Satanists are mostly atheists in reality. Dillon had invented his own new, very jumbled, brand of Satanism. The boy was extremely unstable and troubled – probably experiencing a state of drug-induced psychosis, but he wasn't a murderer. But his actions were becoming increasingly dangerous, to him and others. Hunter also seemed suspicious, you yourself told me on the phone that he was acting weird, and his criminal past shone a very bad light on him. But again, he wasn't the one responsible for the killings, was he? Everyone has their secrets, some people are surrounded by them, and a good detective peels them away one by one till they get to the truth – or as near to it as possible. Listen, maybe going through all this will help you in the future – you'll always remember how you feel right now, and take things slowly and carefully from now on, I'll bet my hat on it.'

'You're not wearing a bloody hat,' Shirley said with a chuckle. 'Thanks though. I know what you mean.' She thought back to the conversation she'd had with Dillon's mum that day, when the poor woman had come to see the site of her son's murder. Yes, what Paul was saying about drug-induced psychosis made sense. Dillon had been falling further and further into his own world, losing touch with reality, and this went some way to explaining his bizarre notes about Eleanor.

And regarding her future work, she thought – well – she couldn't complain. Business had picked up, even over the last two days. Mr Parkhurst had U-turned on his opinion of her, after he'd heard how she'd found out the truth about Eleanor for him; he'd paid her the full whack and had even found the time to leave a glowing review of her agency on Google. He'd stopped short of actually apologising, but when she'd talked to him for over an hour on the phone on Saturday evening, relating and explaining everything that had gone on, his tone had been imbued with respect for her, rather than condescending disdain. As well as shock and grief, of course. That was the part of her job she didn't enjoy, having to tell clients information that upset them, traumatised them. But at least he knew the truth now, and could start grieving for his daughter properly; put everything to rest. If that was at all possible under the fucking awful circumstances.

She looked at Paul.

'Noah did good on this job, bless him,' she said. 'Really surprised me, that boy. I didn't think he'd be able to stick it, but he did.'

'What's he doing now?' Paul said. 'I thought you might bring him with you today. Treat him to a cake and a sandwich.' He smiled as he said this.

'No, he's doing what makes him most happy,' Shirley said. 'Tidying. My desk, to be exact.' She'd finally given him permission that morning, after making sure her closely guarded file was nowhere in the vicinity. She didn't think she'd ever show him – or anyone else for that matter – what was in it, but you never knew. The right moment might arise, but she'd doubted it. Yes, Noah had turned out to be a good egg, a real trooper. And he'd said he was already looking forward to their next case, much to his mother's alarm. Gloria had come to visit them yesterday, and had oscillated between admiration for her son's role in the case and fury at Shirley for putting him in such a dangerous situation. Nevertheless, by the time she was leaving she'd seemed cautiously pleased that Noah was doing something that interested him at last...

And she'd noticed another thing; she'd become so caught up with the case that she hadn't thought about Tiffany much at all over the last day. The fact that she'd left still hurt, she still missed her – hadn't heard from her at all since she'd walked out – but that was okay. She was at peace with it now. Was actually glad all the arguments were over. And she was in no rush to meet anyone else, not for the moment.

'Anyway,' Shirley said, draining the last dregs of her coffee. 'I better make a move in a minute.'

'Got somewhere better to be, have you?' Paul said with a grin.

'Yep,' Shirley said with a smile, putting down her mug. 'No offence, love, but there's a hospital patient I promised to go and see...'

60

As she entered the ward, Shirley saw Seth's pale face lying back against a pillow. His arm stuck out from under a blanket, and his hand was tightly clasped by another visitor's. Natalie. She was sitting in a chair next to his bed; her expression was serious, but there was a touch of resolve in it too. *I'm here to stay*, it seemed to say. *Like it or not, I'm here to look after Seth.*

He gave a weak smile as Shirley approached.

'How you doing, Seth?' Shirley said with a smile, holding out an enormous box of chocolates. 'Shall I put these on the trolley over there with all your other goodies?'

'Yes please,' Seth said. His voice was strained, barely recognisable. Bandages encompassed his neck, and Shirley tried not to imagine the state it must be in now. Cuts and bruises danced across every bit of Seth's skin she could see; that bastard Weatherby had really tried to end the boy's life for good, had put a lot of effort into destroying him. She would be eternally glad that he hadn't quite managed to.

'I'm very glad to see that you're on the mend,' Shirley said, her tone gentle. She planted her feet securely next to the bed – it looked like she was going to have to stand for the duration of her visit as Natalie was in full command of the only chair and wasn't showing any signs of getting up – but no matter, she wasn't planning on staying too long. She'd just wanted to see for herself that Seth had pulled through his horrendous ordeal at the hands of Weatherby; she'd felt so helpless having to wait outside the cottage that night, knowing that any amount of terrible things could be being inflicted on Seth, with her just a few metres away. Needed to see with her own eyes that he was okay now. 'How are you feeling?'

Seth managed a small grin.

'I've been better,' he said, his voice a rasp. 'But I'm alive, and that's the main thing. The doctors say I'll have a scar on my neck for the rest of my life. I might be able to have surgery on it in the future, but I think I might leave it as it is. It's a war wound. And it will always remind me about how going through all of this has changed me; hopefully for the better.'

'Yes, most definitely,' Shirley said, nodding. 'You're a tough cookie, Seth. You should be very proud of yourself.'

Seth looked at her, then looked away. Shirley thought she saw a glisten of a tear in his eye. *For God's sake, change the subject you idiot*, she told herself. *You didn't come here to make the boy cry, did you?*

'Er, have you had many visitors, Seth?' she said, looking from him to Natalie. 'It certainly looks like you have.'

'Yes, there's been quite a few.' Natalie gestured towards the hospital trolley that was laden with flowers, fruit, cards, teddies, and now Shirley's box of chocolates. 'Even Hunter came by this morning.' She looked down, but then looked up again to meet Shirley's gaze, a touch of defiance in her eyes.

'Ah, that's nice,' Shirley said, making sure her tone was neutral and pleasant. 'How did it go?'

There was a pause. Natalie looked at Seth.

'It was a bit awkward, actually,' she said, then smiled. Her pinched little face totally changed; for a second it shone with sunny humour. 'But I'm glad he did.'

'So am I,' Seth said, his words coming out slowly. 'He told us about his past – his time in prison, about why he'd got so stressed when you started investigating Eleanor's death. We were both shocked, weren't we?' Natalie nodded. 'It was a lot to take in. And it explained his crazy behaviour recently. He was worried he was going to go down for a crime he didn't do because of his past. I think he was starting to lose his marbles about it, actually. But I'm glad he was honest and told us the truth in the end. He was a good friend to me, and I'll always be grateful to him for that.'

'Good.' Shirley nodded. 'I'm glad.'

'Hunter said he's putting his studies on hold for a bit,' Natalie said, shifting forward. 'He said the way his brain got messed up when Eleanor died made him realise he's not quite ready for university life just yet, that he still needs to come to terms with himself and what he's done. He saw Eleanor that night, you know? After he left the bar. He could see she was upset, and he asked her if she wanted to come back to his room for a drink, but she said no. I think he fancied her if I'm honest. In fact, I know he did, the way I caught him looking at her. After that he said his memories started getting confused; he was mixing up his rape of the girl years ago with meeting Eleanor on Wednesday night, he started worrying he'd done the same to her. Hunter said the other evening things got so bad he walked all the way to the Tingewick Wood and started smashing up branches with his axe. He'd taken his woodcarving up a step, and decided to destroy some wood instead of creating art from it. That's when he realised he needed to get right away from here, before he went completely off his rocker. So he's going travelling for a few months. I think he said he'd start with Norway. Probably because he loves Vikings. And he gave Seth his most prized possession today – the figurine of Odin he carved a few months ago. It's over there on the trolley.'

'Yeah,' Seth said, looking at it. 'He said that Odin is the Norse god of wisdom and magic, and figured I could do with a bit of both of those things right now.'

Shirley smiled, looking over at the wooden figure. It was superb; Hunter definitely had a talent.

'Well, that is good news,' she said. 'And I can see you're in very good hands here, Seth.' She winked at Natalie, who grinned back. 'Right, I won't bother you for much longer, I just wanted to make sure you were all right. You're a strong person, Seth. What happened to you the other night was fucking awful, excuse the language. But I can see you're going to be okay. And I'm very glad about that.'

A few minutes later, Shirley was walking back across the hospital car park. As she opened the door of her car, she felt her phone bleep into life in her pocket.

'Detective Shirley Butterworth?' a woman's voice said, when she answered it. 'I'm so glad I've got hold of you. You come very highly recommended. It's my daughter. She's missing. Can you help me find her?'

As Shirley chatted to the panicked woman, a feeling of contentment washed through her. During the last few days she'd proved to herself she had the necessary qualities to go forward in her business with her head held high. She might not be the brains of Britain but she had what was needed in that department. And she'd chosen perseverance over alcohol, which had surprised and pleased her no end. Well, well, well, there was a first for everything! But the greatest sensation she'd felt throughout the investigation was passion; she'd had the essential gumption and drive, curiosity and hunger for truth and justice that had compelled her through to the end of it, sometimes through hard knock-backs and disappointments. At last, she was a proper, respectable private detective. And bloody hell – it felt good.

232

THE END

ACKNOWLEDGEMENTS

Thanks so much to the Bloodhound Books staff for helping to bring *Devil's Play* out into the world, particularly Betsy, Fred, Tara, Hannah and, of course, Ian for his wonderful editing. Thanks to the ARC readers for giving it their time and attention. And thank you to Rich, Bethan, Olivia, Ben, my mother and all my friends, for being generally amazing.

A NOTE FROM THE PUBLISHER

Thank you for reading this book. If you enjoyed it please do consider leaving a review on Amazon to help others find it too.

We hate typos. All of our books have been rigorously edited and proofread, but sometimes mistakes do slip through. If you have spotted a typo, please do let us know and we can get it amended within hours.

info@bloodhoundbooks.com

9 781914 614576